First published by
Scholastic Australia in 2012

ISBN 978-0-545-53736-0

12 11 10 9 8 7 6 5 4 3 2 1   12 13 14 15 16 17/0

                                            40

Printed in the U.S.A.

This edition first printing, December 2012

Internal photography:
note paper © iStockphoto.com/tomograf
coffee cup stain © iStockphoto.com/BingoPixel

Typeset in Agfa Wile

For Gabrielle-san,
Damian-san, Chantelle-san,
and Jacqui-san - SW

To Ed: Front Window Ninja
(no need for the barking, but
we appreciate your constant
vigilance!) - HM

1

THE 49TH _unauthorized_ EVACUATION
∧

A ninja must never use lethal force unless
a) he has exhausted all other possibilities,
b) not to do so could bring about his own demise,
or c) he really, _really_ wants to.

The Ninja Warrior's Handbook, Volume 27

The bomb was set to go off in the kindergarten classroom at three o'clock. This was designed to cause maximum carnage. Three o'clock was pick-up time, so the kindergarten would be packed full of parents and siblings, caregivers, grandparents and nannies, all admiring the students' artwork, again. If the bomb exploded there would be blood, guts and papier-mâché everywhere . . . OK, so it wasn't actually that kind of bomb, but it still meant toxic **NASAL DOOM** to anyone within a five kilometer radius. It was a

PAINT-STRIPPING, NOSTRIL-HAIR-SINGEING, GALAXY-GRADE, STINK BOMB!

The stink bomb had been delivered to the school in the morning mail and the janitor, Mr. Janitor, carried it to the classroom. The janitor's name wasn't really Mr. Janitor, but because no one could remember his real name, everyone just called him that. And as Mr. Janitor was widely regarded as the grumpiest person on the planet (he would leap about like a frog on a barbecue if he found trash in the playground) no one had the courage to ask him his real name in case he got so angry he burst.

When he delivered the package to the kindergarten class, Mr. Janitor did think it was weird that it was ticking. But it wasn't his job to check whether packages contained stink bombs or not. Oh no, that would take all day! His job was simply to do the deliveries, pick up paper in the playground and, whenever possible, get really, *really* angry. If they wanted him to start checking packages for bombs then they would have to start paying him more. Also, Mr. Janitor

was ~~dishlexik~~ ~~dizylecksick~~ not a good reader. If he had been then he would have noticed that the outside of the parcel was labeled:

Mr. Janitor marched into the kindergarten class, dumped the package on Ms. Bottomley's desk, grunted, then marched right out again.

Fortunately for the kindergartners, Ms. Bottomley *could* read (she'd been to university and stuff) and as soon as she realized what was inside the **PUNGENT** package, she ordered the class to evacuate.

Unfortunately for the kindergartners, the principal, Mr. Kinkoffen, was in charge of all evacuations and when he saw Ms. Bottomley in her snazzy red fire warden's helmet, marching her students outside, he hurried over and marched them all right back in again.

Despite Ms. Bottomley's protests that the classroom was beginning to **REEK LIKE A SKUNK'S ARMPIT AFTER PE**, Mr. Kinkoffen was a stickler for procedure and this case was not going to change that. It was his job to run the fire drills, and he simply could not allow an unauthorized evacuation, especially not without his whistle. It went against school policy. He would certainly have words with Ms. Bottomley about this later. He might even demote her from fire warden, or tell her to take a week off, just to teach her a lesson. Maybe he'd send her off on an all-expenses-paid world cruise. That would show her who was in charge of evacuations! One thing the school ought to get right was its fire drills. Heck, they'd had forty-eight fire drills this term alone, and it was only week three.

4

Mr. Kinkoffen sat the students down to lecture them on the importance of authorized evacuations, while Ms. Bottomley sat at her desk, watching the ticking package and biting her fingernails. She crinkled her nose in disgust as the plants on her desk tried to crawl out of the room (which was a bit weird really, seeing how they were plastic). She tried to complain but Mr. Kinkoffen held up his hand to silence her. He would *certainly* be having words with Ms. Bottomley in the staffroom. Yes. Strong words. He might even have to stand on an upturned milk crate while having his strong words with her, just to show her who was ~~taller~~ the boss.

Finally, one of the students got up the courage to raise his hand.

Mr. Kinkoffen pointed at the boy with the curly red hair. He wasn't very good at remembering students' names and tended to use their hairstyles as a memory aid. "Yes, the boy with the curly red hair."

"Excuse me, sir," said the boy with the curly red hair. "But there's a **STINK BOMB** in the classroom. Don't we need to get out?"

"Don't be silly," chuckled Mr. Kinkoffen. "No bombs are allowed on the school premises. Not without authorization."

Another student raised his hand. His head was completely bald because he'd recently had lice.

"Yes, the boy whose head is completely bald because he recently had lice?"

"Sir," said the boy, pulling his sweater over his nose. "There really is a stink bomb."

Mr. Kinkoffen smiled. Honestly! The imagination of these kindergarten students. It was priceless. He could hardly wait until they reached high school, by which time imagination would more or less have been sucked out of them.

"Look, sir," said another boy whose hair stuck up as though he'd been playing with an electrical socket. He pointed over to Ms. Bottomley's desk.

Mr. Kinkoffen's smile froze on his face. He looked at the ticking package on the desk. His eyesight wasn't the best so he squinted to make out the writing, which to him looked like this:

6

"And is it an authorized stink bomb?" he asked no one in particular.

Ms. Bottomley adjusted her fire warden helmet. "Please, may I evacuate the building now, Mr. Kinkoffen?"

"Not so fast, Bottomley," he replied. "I want to first make sure that this is a proper bomb and not a hoax. May I?" Mr. Kinkoffen pointed to Ms. Bottomley's computer.

"Yes," she snapped, as her nose hairs desperately tried to find a way of sealing her nasal passages.

While Mr. Kinkoffen was engrossed in the task of Googling authorized bombs, Ms. Bottomley quickly and quietly snuck the kindergartners back outside to safety. Unauthorized evacuation or not, her duty of care was to her students. That was one of the things they drilled into you during teacher training.

RULES FOR TEACHERS #1052

Under no circumstances are you to allow your students to be blown over by toxic stink gas. This includes exposure to a) authorized or unauthorized stink bombs, and b) accidental or intentional passing of wind.

"Mmmnnn," said Mr. Kinkoffen to the empty classroom a short while later. "If the label on the package has an accurate description of the contents, then it appears as though we do indeed have a legitimate stink bomb. It's made by the **MEGA-BLAST CORPORATION**.

According to their website, if this particular device was detonated it would blow over everything within a five kilometer radius. In that case I think I will order an evacuation onto the playground. First, however, I would like a couple of volunteers to walk briskly—no running!—to my office to retrieve my whistle."

Mr. Kinkoffen looked up from the computer at the classroom of empty chairs. "Ms. Bottomley! Ms. Bottomley! Come back at once! I haven't officially authorized the evacuation yet!" Mr. Kinkoffen made a strange harrumph noise, the sort a short donkey might make if it wandered off a tall cliff. Then he shouted at the empty room. "Everyone, return to your desks immediately!"

Mr. Kinkoffen shook his head and sighed. Honestly! That woman! This really was unacceptable. And a terrible example to the students. Perhaps two weeks off and two world cruises were in order!

THE DT CLUB

When jumping backwards into a tree, a ninja should check first for the presence of birds or other ninjas. A startled bird could give away your location, and another ninja might get annoyed if you land on him.

The Ninja Warrior's Handbook, Volume 27

"That's all? You got a lunchtime DT just for writing a story?" asked Jake Chen, who was in detention (DT) himself for arguing with his Science teacher that turtles were reptiles and not amphibians.

Ben Clarkeson scratched his head. He was supposed to be at a trumpet lesson now but instead he was stuck in the boring time-out room with Mr. Caruthers and the DT crew because of his creative writing exercise.

"Mr. Kinkoffen said that I shouldn't have

used real people's names, especially his. He also made me go and show Ms. Bottomley."

"What did *she* say?"

"It was weird, but when she got to the bit about Mr. Kinkoffen making the students go back into the classroom with the stink bomb, she made this snorting noise, kind of like a pig eating granola, and ran off to the staffroom with my story. Then I heard this other noise through the wall, like someone was tickling a sack full of hyenas, and when she came back she had tears running down her cheeks. I thought maybe she was upset because I used her real name too, or that she was worried about her students getting stink-bombed and stuff."

"I tell you," said Jake Chen. "Teachers are weird."

"I heard that, Jake Chen!" snapped Mr. Caruthers, who was in charge of the DT crew. Mr. Caruthers was extremely tall. He was so tall he had to walk with a stoop to avoid being decapitated by the ceiling fans.

Mr. Caruthers stared at the two boys over the top of his glasses with a **LEVEL-2** glare.

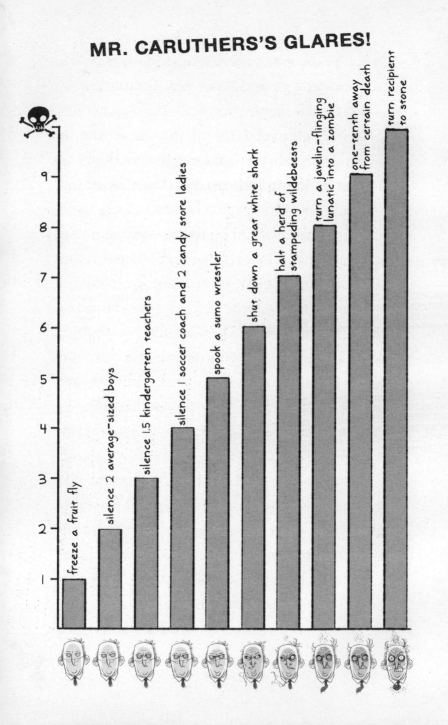

A **LEVEL-2** glare wasn't that intense but it was enough to silence the sixth-graders. Mr. Caruthers was rather proud of his glares which he'd perfected over forty years of teaching. It was far more effective than the strap, or the cane, or dangling kids upside down from the bell tower by their ankles as teachers used to do in the ~~good~~ old days. Yes, he was proud of his glares alright.

The highest glare he'd ever used was a **LEVEL-8** which he'd directed at a rather unruly student in the 1970s and who is still, even now, not fully recovered. The student, Frazier Mayheming, had attempted to bring down a passing news helicopter by throwing a javelin at it. Fortunately for the pilot and the news crew, but unfortunately for Mr. Moses (the religious education teacher), Mayheming wildly overestimated his javelin-hurling ability. Rather than spearing the helicopter's rotor blades and sending the chopper spinning out of control into the principal's office, the javelin sailed briefly through the air in an arc before spearing Mr. Moses through his foot and pinning him to the ground.

The language that Mr. Moses directed at Mayheming that day was definitely not what you would expect of a religious education teacher. When Mr. Caruthers arrived on the scene he stormed over to Mayheming and hit him with a **LEVEL-8**. Such was the intensity of Mr. Caruthers's glare that when the ambulance arrived, Frazier Mayheming had to be placed in an induced coma.

Mr. Moses left the teaching profession that afternoon, and as soon as his foot healed he changed careers completely and became an abalone diver. He preferred to take his chances with man-eating great white sharks rather than fourth-grade javelin-flinging lunatics like Mayheming.

"This isn't the first time one of my stories has landed me in trouble," said Ben Clarkeson, "but I've never had detention before. What do we have to do?"

"We just sit here," said Jake Chen. Like Ben, Jake was a **MEGA-BRAIN**, an **ULTRA-**

NERD, but, according to every teacher he'd ever had, sometimes he was "too smart for his own good." Whatever that meant. "We just sit here," Jake repeated, "and try to avoid **THE GLARE**."

Ben Clarkeson looked around the classroom. Apart from himself and Jake Chen there was one other sixth-grader on DT—Veejay Cameron (which surprised Ben), and fourth-grader Hugo Frog-Morton (which did not surprise Ben). Veejay Cameron sat there humming to himself, while Hugo Frog-Morton grumbled like a distant earthquake. There was also some ancient guy in the back corner who'd been lodged there for so long that everyone just ignored him.

Hugo Frog-Morton had done something so bad that no one was even allowed to talk about it. But that didn't stop the rumors from spreading. One story was that he'd created a deadly disease using one of his PE socks and a particularly lethal fart, which he'd kept stored in a jar for years. Another had him creating a black hole—for disposing either an annoying teacher or a bad midyear report—using the same jar and an egg beater. No one knew what the real story was because no one was able to speak to Frog-Morton without him biting them. Just last week the school counselor had tried to have a chat with him about his behavior and now she was in the hospital with rabies.

Hugo Frog-Morton had been stuck in fourth grade for so long that it was impossible to imagine fourth grade without him. Another rumor going around was that the reason he couldn't advance to Year Five (apart from the fact that he didn't know the difference between an elephant and a goose) was that his father was still in Year Five and it was against school policy to pass your parents.

"What did you do?" Ben asked Jake.

"I got into another argument with Mrs. Attenborough. Told her that a turtle was a reptile and not an amphibian."

"But a turtle *is* a reptile," said Ben.

"I know," said Jake Chen.

"So you got detention for being right?"

"Well . . . that and throwing a moldy orange at her butt when she was writing something on the board . . . But it was an accident, I swear."

"Riiiight," said Ben, "how'd you do that?"

Jake sighed. "I was aiming at the bin . . . and I don't know . . . that butt must have its own gravitational pull or something because the orange curved and smacked straight into her. Bull's eye!"

"What about you?" whispered Ben to Veejay Cameron. "What are you in for?"

"*Noth-ing,*" said Veejay in a singsong voice, without looking up from his book.

"He just likes to come in here and read," explained Jake. He leaned in towards Ben and whispered, "His mom hangs around outside the school making sure that he's had his lunch, done all his work, got his socks pulled up, blown his nose, covered the toilet seat with twenty-seven rolls of toilet paper. The guy just needs a break."

Ben remembered his first day at St. Hall's. His mom had pulled his pants up so high that she'd practically given him a wedgie. Luckily she'd backed off a bit over the years. "I heard Pongo's supposed to be in here too," Ben added.

Something outside the classroom window had caught Jake's eye. He stared out over towards

Brandon House where three men in orange jackets were skulking about. One guy was pushing a wheelbarrow and glancing around as he adjusted the blue tarp that was covering his load. "Who are those guys?" he asked Ben.

"I don't know," said Ben. "But they've been hanging around for days. Looks like they're up to something bad."

"*SUBSISTO SERMO!*" snapped Mr. Caruthers.

"What?" said Ben.

"It means 'stop talking' in Latin," whispered Jake.

Ben scratched his head. "But I'm *not* talking in Latin."

"*Ego sum iens ut vestigium volvo,*" continued Mr. Caruthers.

Ben looked over at Jake again. "What was that about a Volvo?"

"He's going to mark the roll," said Jake.

"Jake Chen?"

"Here, Mr. Caruthers, sir."

"Ben Clarkeson?"

"Sir."

"Hugo Frog-Morton?"

Nothing.

"Hugo Frog-Morton? If you're here, grunt once for yes."

The creature known as Hugo let out a sort of deep, guttural growl, kind of like a hippo burping.

"Close enough," said Mr. Caruthers. "Frazier Mayheming?"

Ben and Jake instantly turned to the back corner where the mysterious ancient guy was sitting. "That's Frazier Mayheming?" hissed Ben. Mayheming was wearing a faded and ridiculously small school uniform, and mumbling something about javelins and helicopters being stupid.

"FRAZIER MAYHEMING!" snapped Mr. Caruthers, ratcheting up the volume and getting ready to unleash one of his glares. Surely he wouldn't hit Mayheming with another one, not after the induced coma incident, thought Ben.

"Here," grunted the ancient dude while Jake and Ben stared at each other with their jaws hanging open. Frazier Mayheming had committed his crimes against javelins (and religious education teachers) in the seventies—the *nineteen-seventies*—and he was still here on DT!

"And finally, Pongo Twistleton?"

"He's not here, sir," said Jake. "He's . . . running—"

"Late?" sighed Mr. Caruthers, rolling his eyes. *"Quis a admiratio."*

"That means what a sur—" began Jake, but Ben cut him off.

"Even I can guess what that means: 'What a surprise.'"

THE LATE PONGO

The first rule of the ninja is that if the sword is unsheathed it must draw blood, if not of your adversary's, then your own. A small shaving nick will suffice.

The Ninja Warrior's Handbook, Volume 27

Pongo Twistleton was running late because, well, Pongo Twistleton was always running late. Sometimes it was his fault, but today it wasn't. Not really. Unless you want to blame him for having demented brothers.

When Pongo woke up this morning he was surprised to find himself tied upside down in a tree. Actually, he wasn't that surprised at all. Not really. So far this year he'd woken up in a tree 73 times. What surprised him, though, was that the tree was moving at over 100 kilometers an hour. That's not the sort of thing you would

normally expect from a coconut tree. Even a coconut tree in a hurricane. As it turns out, the tree's owners were moving interstate and they'd hired a moving company to take the tree with them.

So what was Pongo doing strapped upside down in a tree when he should have been on lunchtime DT for being late? To put it simply, Pongo's brothers were mad. They were six years older than Pongo, and their names were Tweedle-dumb and Tweedle-even-dumber. Even their own father reckoned if they kept skipping school then the only jobs they'd be able to get would be working in a shopping center parking lot. As speed bumps.

Unfortunately for Pongo, the Tweedles loved playing practical jokes. Unfortunately for Pongo, the person that the Tweedles liked playing practical jokes on best of all was him. And to make matters even worse, Pongo was a deep, deep sleeper.

So far this year Pongo had woken up dangling over a cliff in his sleeping bag, in the refrigerated goods section of an Antarctic-

bound scientific research vessel, stuffed inside a barrel as it hurtled over Niagara Falls, and trapped in a shopping cart that the Tweedles were pushing up the side of an active volcano. There was also that time when he woke up next to an angry ostrich in the cargo section of a plane bound for the wilds of Africa. He'd been very late for school on that day indeed.

"I would like to apologize for my tardiness, sir," said Pongo, **BOING-BOING-BOING-ING** into the classroom on his pogo stick.

"Let me guess," said Mr. Caruthers, squinting at the leaves poking out of Pongo's hair. "Something to do with a tree."

"Affirmative, sir," said Pongo, giving his head a shake. "Indeed, the fastest coconut tree on the planet!" He maneuvered his pogo stick into position and then plunked himself down at the desk behind his friends Jake and Ben.

So there they were, all seven of them:

1. Mr. Caruthers, the tallest speaker of Latin in the world and possessor of a lethal set of glares.

2. Jake Chen, who knew that a turtle was a reptile, not an amphibian, and that if you threw a moldy orange anywhere near Mrs. Attenborough (or maybe even in the opposite direction) it would slam into her buttocks.

3. Ben Clarkeson, who liked playing the trumpet and writing stories about stink bomb scares and strange school principals.

4. Pongo Twistleton, the late Pongo Twistleton, who had recently decided that he was allergic to the world and now went everywhere **BOING-BOING-BOINGING** on a pogo stick.

5. Veejay Cameron, who wanted to be an opera singer and who didn't have to be in DT at all but was hiding from his mommy.

6. Hugo Frog-Morton, who'd done something so awfully bad that no one knew what it was.

7. And the infamous Frazier Mayheming, who'd been sentenced to DT, life without parole.

All in all it seemed like just an ordinary day on lunchtime DT at St. Hall's Boys' Grammar. But what the DT boys didn't know was that four of them were about to become ninjas.

ST. HALL'S HALL HALL

A ninja warrior must always come to the aid of
the weak unless a) he happens not to like the
weak very much, or b) the weak are being
picked on by Hugo Frog-Morton.

The Ninja Warrior's Handbook, Volume 27

The following day Ben, Jake and Pongo rounded a corner (or in Pongo's case **BOINGED** around) and found Hugo Frog-Morton sitting on an upturned trash bin.

This was only part of the problem. They quickly realized that they were in the wrong corridor (or *hall* as it was called) at the wrong time and would probably score another DT if they couldn't explain themselves.

The assembly hall at St. Hall's was called "the hall." And the corridor outside St. Hall's hall (which is where they were) was called

"the hallway," which was usually shortened to "the hall." Although St. Hall's hall was out of bounds during lunch, St. Hall's hall hall wasn't. It just took too much explaining, so it was best not to get caught there.

Ben, Jake and Pongo stared at Hugo Frog-Morton. A strange murmuring hung in the air.

"Er," said Ben and stopped. Frog-Morton didn't move. Had he even noticed them?

Although they were in Year Six and Frog-Morton was only in Year Four, they were all a little nervous around him. In fact, the whole school was a little nervous around Frog-Morton. Heck, a homicidally deranged leopard would be a little nervous around Frog-Morton. He could infect you with his homemade diseases, or rear up without warning like a cobra and bite. And then you would either die or be forced to visit the school nurse who would amputate the infected area, which would be a serious bummer, especially if he happened to bite you on your head.

Finally it was Jake who got up the courage

to say something. "Why are you sitting on top of that trash bin?"

Hugo Frog-Morton looked down at the bin and then glared at the three of them. "I'm not," he snarled. "I'm sitting on the *bottom* of it."

"Okay, then," said Pongo, as he leaned against the wall on his pogo stick. "Why are you sitting on the bottom of a trash bin?"

"Because I don't like opera."

The three friends looked at each other. It seemed as if Frog-Morton had finally gone barking mad. He didn't like opera so here he was perched on top of an upturned trash bin? What did he do to protest against homework? Dress up in a chicken suit and dance around a barn?

"Riiiiight," said Ben.

"Right," said Pongo.

"Are you completely nuts?" said Jake, who, unlike everyone else, wasn't afraid of anything.

"It wasn't opera," came a muffled singsong voice.

"Who was that?" asked Ben.

"Him," said Hugo.

The three of them looked around. There was no one else about.

"Him who?" asked Pongo.

Hugo sighed. "That kid who's always singing opera."

"Veejay Cameron?" said Ben.

"He came twirling down Hall's hall hall," snarled Hugo, "singing about the hills being alive."

"See," came that muffled singsong voice again. "It wasn't opera. It was from *The Sound of Music*, which everyone knows is a musical."

Hugo ignored Veejay. "So I stuffed him in here and sat on the bottom of it." He gave the side of the bin a swift kick just to hammer home the point.

"Ouch!" sang the bin.

Jake wheeled himself up to the bin and knocked on the side. "Are you really in there, Veejay?"

"Yeee–es."

Jake knocked again. "What's it like?"

"Daaa–ark."

The funny thing was, Veejay didn't seem to have any complaints about being stuffed in a trash bin. He didn't seem upset at all. His voice suggested that it was perfectly normal for anyone who twirled down corridors (or Hall's hall hall) reciting musicals to, sooner or later, find themselves stuffed in an upturned trash bin. And Veejay could easily have stopped Hugo Frog-Morton from stuffing him in there, just by . . . well, sitting on him. Veejay was

so enormous that the ground shook when he walked. He was like the Alps. He even had a snow-capped peak. Okay, it was probably just a bit of dandruff on top of his head, but still.

Ben cautiously joined Jake by the bin, wary in case Hugo should suddenly bare his fangs. He rapped the side of the bin. "Can we get you anything, Veejay?"

There was a pause while Veejay considered this.

Ben, Jake and Pongo looked up at Hugo Frog-Morton who growled and shook his head.

"Veejay?" repeated Ben.

"A book light?"

"You have a book in there?" asked Ben.

"Of course!"

"How can you read it?" said Jake.

"I *caaa-an't*," sang Veejay as Hugo growled again. "That's why I need a *booo-hook* light."

Hugo gave the bin another swift kick.

Pongo boinged backwards. "Let's go," he hissed to his friends. "Let's find out what those strange men in orange jackets are doing."

Jake had a highly tuned sense of right and wrong. Now that he was involved, he couldn't just walk . . . okay, *wheel* away. He couldn't stand there . . . okay, *sit* there, while a weaker . . . okay, *stronger* (this is getting tiring) kid was being bullied by someone stronger . . . okay, *weaker*. He glanced at his friends. Ben was fiddling with his trumpet valve. Pongo was bouncing on his pogo stick, ready to bound far, far away from Hugo and his singing bin captive. Jake had to think of something quickly. But what?

Veejay's constant, painful singing was not helping him come up with a plan!

Jake suddenly noticed that Hugo was getting angrier and angrier and redder and redder each time Veejay hit a certain high note.

"I have an idea," whispered Jake through the hard plastic.

"I'm all *eaaa-ears*," sang Veejay.

"GRRRRRRR!" screeched Frog-Morton.

"Keep singing," ordered Jake.

"*Ah-ha,*" sang Veejay. "A request!"

"GRRRRRRR!"

"Sing something really annoying," continued Jake. "I mean really *really* annoying."

"Are you nuts?" Ben hissed at Jake. "Frog-Morton will go beserk!"

"Exactly," whispered Jake. "Look. He's not going to let Veejay out, so we have to help him."

Ben and Pongo looked unconvinced.

"Come on, we have to do something. Anyway, I think Hugo's forgotten that we're even here."

"The upside and downside," said Ben, "of being a nerd . . ."

Pongo sighed. "If we mess up," he said, "there's a very real possibility that we might get Veejay killed."

"That's a chance I'm prepared to take," said Jake.

"What was that?" came Veejay's muffled voice.

"Um, nothing," said Jake. "Just hurry up and start singing," he added, figuring that whatever Veejay sang would be annoying to Hugo Frog-Morton (or anything with ears). "But make sure you sing it really *really* high."

"What would you like me to *siii–ing*?" replied Veejay.

Hugo Frog-Morton growled again and thumped the bin. "How about you sing, 'My name is Veejay Cameron, and if I sing another note I'll die'?"

There was a moment's silence from the bin. "In which key?"

"GRRRRRR!"

"What was the last musical you were in?" whispered Jake, trying not to stir the beast above.

The bin thought for a moment. "The Hills' District Amateur Theatrical and Musical Society's production of *South Pacific*."

"Perfect," said Jake, although he had no idea what the bin was talking about.

"Do you know how hard it is to get a B-29 bomber into a senior citizen's hall?" mumbled Veejay. "Not to mention the two hundred cubic meters of sand."

"Don't worry about any of that!" hissed Jake. "Just sing something from it. Hurry!"

"What?"

"Anything!"

"Which act?"

For a moment Jake could almost see why Hugo Frog-Morton wanted to shove Veejay Cameron in a trash bin. "It doesn't matter!"

"It does to me."

"Okay then," interjected Ben before they all died of old age. "Act one!"

"Act one it is." There was silence from the bin, followed by the sound of rummaging, then a squirt of what sounded like air freshener.

Jake looked at Ben. "Don't ask."

They heard Veejay clear his throat. "Doh ray mei. Mei mei mei. Fah so la tee tee tee tee doh."

"That's from *The Sound of Music*!" said Ben, who knew more about musicals than he was prepared to admit.

"You are correct," said Veejay. "But I'm just limbering up the old vocal chords."

"Do you want to die?" hissed Jake. "Do you want us *all* to die?"

"Oh don't be silly," replied Veejay. "Hugo won't kill me over a little doh-ray-me-ing."

"No," snarled Jake. "But *we* might."

"Quick," encouraged Ben. "Sing something!"

"Okay then," said Veejay. "How about Bali Ha'i?"

"Whatever!" said Ben. "I mean, perfect!" Ben still wasn't entirely sure where Jake was going with this, and he didn't know anything about Bali Ha'is, but it certainly beat the three of them sitting on Hugo Frog-Morton and running the risk of being bitten.

"Mei mei mei . . ." sang Veejay.

"GGGRRR!" growled Hugo.

"That'll do! Just do that higher!" encouraged Jake. "You have to sing it higher!"

". . . MEI MEI MEI!" Veejay's voice went higher and higher.

"GGGGGRRRRRRR!!!!!"

"Keep going!" urged Jake.

"MEI MEI MEI!!!!" Now Veejay's pitch was almost above the threshold of the human audio range. Dogs within fifteen kilometers of the school grounds suddenly began barking and whimpering.

Meanwhile Hugo Frog-Morton was getting madder and madder.

"GGGGGGGGGRRRRRRRRRR!!!"

"MEI!" sang (if you could call it that)
Veejay.

Suddenly all the glasses in the staffroom
shattered.

"GGGGGGGGGGRRRRRRR!!!!"

"Quick!" screamed Jake. "He's going to blow.
Run for your lives!"

The three of them ran off down the corridor
to the sound of Ben playing *The Cavalry Charge*
on his trumpet. Actually that's not quite true.
Only Ben ran. Pongo **BOINGED** and Jake
rolled.

When they came to the stairs, Ben bounded
down them two at a time, Pongo **BOINGED**
down them five at a time, while Jake brought
his wheelchair to a controlled crash at the
bottom after taking a flying leap into the abyss
from the top.

In the distance they could hear Veejay's
mei-mei-meing getting higher and higher still!

They could also hear Hugo Frog-Morton's
growls getting deeper and deeper as he
continued to inflate in uncontrollable rage.

"Cover your ears!" yelled Jake. *"MEI MEI MEI MEI MEEEEEE!"*

Veejay pushed the last note so high it could have cut through granite.

No sooner had he hit it than the school building shook on its foundations. This was followed by what sounded suspiciously like internal organs splattering against Hall's hall hall's walls.

Then there was nothing but an eerie silence.

A few minutes later, when the smoke had cleared, they heard a faint, distant and muffled, "Any other requests?"

THE LONG JUMP

Ninjas should always avoid consuming baked beans when on a mission. A direct hit of the methane buildup and discharge could prove lethal, but smaller, accidental doses will merely give away your location.

The Ninja Warrior's Handbook, Volume 27

By the time Jake, Ben and Pongo had retrieved Veejay from the smoldering and melted remnants of the trash bin they were running late for PE.

Jake had decided to keep an eye on Veejay by making him part of their group (whether he liked it or not). That way they could help keep Veejay out of trouble and in return, Jake hoped Veejay's sheer volume might help make their existence known.

On their way to the rugby field, they crept (wheeled, **BOINGED**) past Brandon House

to see if they could spot the mysterious men in orange jackets. Jake was pretty sure he caught a glimpse of the bearded wheelbarrow guy sizing up the library before he slipped out of sight behind Brandon House. Was he trying to get in? What was he hiding in his wheelbarrow, under that blue tarp? He'd better not sneak inside the library and steal anything from the aerospace shelves, thought Jake.

Ben, Jake, Pongo and Veejay tried sneaking onto the rugby field without being seen, but they needn't have bothered.

Even though their entourage included a pogo stick, a wheelchair glinting in the sun, and Veejay's singing which was sending wild-life scurrying for cover, the fact that these four boys were widely regarded as **THE BIGGEST NERDS ON THE PLANET** meant that no one—not even Mr. Snodgrass, their PE teacher—noticed them coming.

Finally Jake tugged on Mr. Snodgrass's rugby shirt.

"Where have you nerds been?" demanded Mr. Snodgrass, suddenly glaring at the four boys. [Note: Mr. Snodgrass was a total rugby nut and for him humanity was divided into two groups: those who could pack down in a scrum, and those who couldn't. And if you couldn't, then you may as well not have existed.]

"Well?" continued Mr. Snodgrass. "I'm waiting. And I'll wait all day if necessary."

"It was Hugo Frog-Morton's fault, sir," said Ben.

Mr. Snodgrass folded his arms and smiled. "What did he do now?"

"He *blew up*, sir," sang Veejay.

Mr. Snodgrass glared up at Veejay. Although Veejay was technically capable of packing down in a scrum, the chances of him ever doing so were less than zero. Unless someone happened to put on a show called, *Rugby: The Musical.* "Blew up?" chuckled Mr. Snodgrass. "Hugo Frog-Morton's always blowing up. Who did he blow up at this time?" Unlike every other teacher at St. Hall's, Mr. Snodgrass liked Hugo Frog-Morton because he was a whiz on the rugby field. Snodgrass didn't care how many nerds or fellow teachers Hugo blew up at. To watch him slalom through the St. Ponsonby's defense on a Saturday morning was truly a sight to behold. Unless, of course, you were part of the St. Ponsonby's defense.

"No, sir," said Jake, wheeling his chair right in front of Mr. Snodgrass. "He really did blow up. Spontaneously combusted."

"Spontaneously combusted?" Mr. Snodgrass scratched his head. "What in the name of holy lineout does that mean?"

"It means he *blew up*, sir," said the four friends together. "Exploded."

"What?" said Mr. Snodgrass. "Completely?"

"Well you can't blow up a bit," said Ben. "You either blow up or you don't."

Mr. Snodgrass bowed his head. "That's awful news. A complete catastrophe. The team will need a new halfback now."

"Riiiiiiight," said Ben.

"Oh, well. Can't be helped," said Mr. Snodgrass. His sentimentality only went so far. "Josh Davis will have to step up. He's ready for the challenge."

"Riiiiiiight," said Ben again.

"Okay," said Mr. Snodgrass. "Whose turn is it?"

Everyone looked over at Mark Fotheringham-Smythe who was standing next to the long jump sandpit holding the rake. He didn't have to rake the pit. Heck, he didn't have to do anything. He was Mark Fotheringham-Smythe—he could do whatever he wanted! It just so happened that he *liked* raking the long jump pit.

Mark Fotheringham-Smythe was the closest thing that St. Hall's had to a god. Tall, tanned, stunningly handsome, impossibly blond. He

was the charismatic captain of everything. Mark was equally at home in the front row of the scrum or back row of the choir. Every time he spoke, the wind seemed to pick up

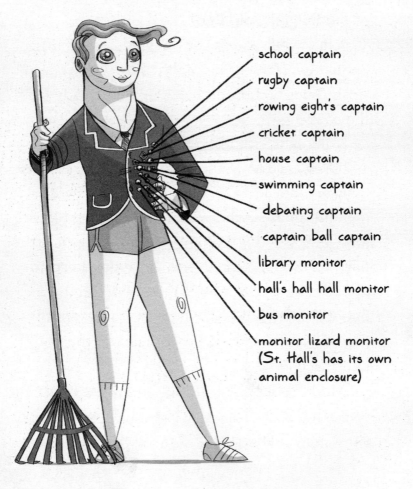

school captain

rugby captain

rowing eight's captain

cricket captain

house captain

swimming captain

debating captain

captain ball captain

library monitor

hall's hall hall monitor

bus monitor

monitor lizard monitor
(St. Hall's has its own
animal enclosure)

and waft through his hair making him appear like a lion atop a rocky outcrop, surveying his kingdom.

"Everybody's had a go, sir," replied Mark Fotheringham-Smythe. The sun glinted off his staggeringly white teeth, practically blinding everyone. "Except for the three nerds."

"*Four* nerds," corrected Jake Chen who then realized what he'd just said.

"Sorry, Jake," corrected Mark. "Four nerds." That was the thing about Mark Fotheringham-Smythe. On top of everything else he was also extremely nice.

He volunteered at an inner city soup kitchen on Saturday nights and spent Sunday mornings reading to the residents of the One Step From Heaven retirement village. The only reason he called Ben and co. nerds was because Mr. Snodgrass did, and he didn't want to correct his teacher. And he said "three" because he didn't want to embarrass Jake by drawing attention to the fact that he couldn't have a turn at the long jump because of his wheelchair and everything.

STUFF MARK FOTHERINGHAM-SMYTHE LIKES

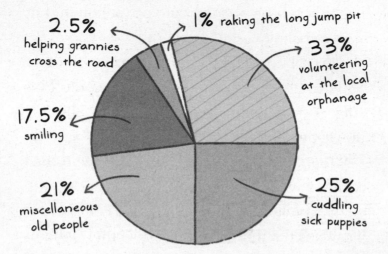

2.5% helping grannies cross the road

1% raking the long jump pit

33% volunteering at the local orphanage

17.5% smiling

21% miscellaneous old people

25% cuddling sick puppies

"Okay!" snapped Mr. Snodgrass. "Let's get this charade over with." Mr. Snodgrass had to give the three of them a go at the long jump. He didn't want their parents showing up at school and accusing him of discriminating against their sons. It was against the rules.

RULES FOR TEACHERS #201847

Do not discriminate against students because of sheer nerdiness. Unless they happen to be smarter than you. In that case, go for it.

Mr. Snodgrass checked his roll. "Veejay Cameron. You're first."

"I can't, sir," sang Veejay, reaching into his backpack. "I have a—"

But Mr. Snodgrass cut him off. "Ah, yes. The famous note. Let's see it then."

Veejay handed Mr. Snodgrass his note. The note was an alphabetical list of things that Veejay was not allowed to do. The note currently ran to twenty-seven pages.

Veejay's mother was a helicopter parent, hovering over Veejay's life so that he couldn't get hurt or in trouble or do anything that might upset him. But the only thing that really seemed to upset Veejay was his mother constantly hovering around. Last year she'd even hired an actual helicopter to hover over the school bus as it carried Veejay and the rest of the Year Fives on a school excursion.

Mr. Snodgrass unfolded Veejay's note, which was so legendary that he'd actually had it published. It came in hardcover, softcover and eBook.

Mr. Snodgrass turned to the note's index.

- Aardvark acquisition, or any activity related to aardvark acquisition and upkeep
- Broad jumping, or other activities that involve inserting Veejay into sand
- Cold storage and cryogenics (no one is to stick Veejay's head into a freezer even if it is a science experiment)
- Dancing or similar activities involving the use of rhythm
- Ectoplasmic inquiries (see also ghosts and ghouls)
- Finger painting
- Ghosts and ghouls (see also ectoplasmic inquiries)
- Hurricane field research
- Igloo construction
- Jetpack experimentation
- Koala keeping (both upkeep and wrangling— those things will urinate on you)
- Llama keeping (both upkeep and wrangling— those things will spit on you)
- Monitor lizard monitoring (both upkeep and wrangling—those things will spit and urinate on you)
- Nectarine gathering (or any activities related to nectarine consumption)

Publisher's Comment: To reproduce the note in its entirety would double the size of this book (at least). We have, however, negotiated with Veejay and his hovering mother to include one excuse from each section.

- October (this is the month of the annual feast of our family god, so Veejay is not permitted to undertake any activity during October)
- Pancakes (there was an incident with a frying pan last time)
- Quilt making (there was an incident with a needle last time)
- Right turns (Veejay prefers to turn left at intersections, so Veejay is banned from any excursions that would require the school bus to turn right)
- Sandcastle construction (see also broad jumping)
- Turtle and/or Tortoise exposure (these are super-sneaky creatures and cannot be trusted)
- Umpteen usage (all non-specific numbers, such as several, lots of, a few, umpteen, numerous, should be replaced by actual integers)
- Vampires. Any reference to vampires (humans or bats) is strictly forbidden in Veejay's presence
- Wishing wells (Veejay has a morbid fear of being thrown into one)
- Xylophones (this one we feel is obvious)

- Yo-yos (under no circumstances is Veejay allowed to venture within ten meters of a deadly yo-yo, unless you want a repeat of the infamous kindergarten incident*)
- Zebras (until someone can determine whether a zebra is a black animal with white stripes or a white animal with black stripes, references to this and other non-specific animals should be avoided in Veejay's presence)

Mr. Snodgrass smiled and scanned the index again just to be certain.

"There's nothing in here saying you're not able to compete in the long jump." Mr. Snodgrass's smile was rapidly turning into a leer.

"I beg your pardon?" said Veejay. He took the note (book) back from Mr. Snodgrass and searched the index. "Here it is under *broad jump*."

"It hasn't been called broad jump in years," said Mr. Snodgrass.

---

*While "playing" with a yo-yo, five-year-old Veejay somehow managed to tie himself, two kindergarten kids, the teacher, the office receptionist, a passing poodle, the principal's pet labradoodle and ten choir kids to the flagpole. It took twelve hours and twenty tailors to untangle.

"It's the same thing," argued Veejay.

"Not to me," said Snodgrass.

"I'll tell my mother," said Veejay.

"Diddums," replied Snodgrass, who was less mature than most of his students. "You're having a turn!"

"Fine!" snapped Veejay. "But I'm certainly not going first."

"I don't care *when* you go," said Mr. Snodgrass. "But you *are* having a go." If they'd wanted to have a go Mr. Snodgrass would have made them sit it out. But because they *didn't* want to have a go, he was determined to make them. He was like that.

RULES FOR TEACHERS #401847
Always make your students have a go at stuff, especially if they don't want to.

Ben Clarkeson decided to go first. He was the most athletic of the four of them. He did win a race at the school swimming carnival

after all. Okay, it was in kindergarten, and okay, yes, it was the dogpaddle, but still.

Ben paced back down the run-up thingy with his trumpet. He marked his run-up all the way to the cricket nets. He figured that long jumping was all about momentum and if he hit the takeoff board thingy after having run all the way from the cricket nets, then the energy that he generated along the way had to hurl him a fair way across the pit. It was simple physics. At least in theory.

Ben took a deep breath, blew his trumpet to let everyone know he was coming, and then tore off. By the time he was about a quarter of the way down the runway he was actually going pretty fast. Unfortunately it was a fair distance from the cricket nets to the long jump pit so around halfway Ben was forced to stop for a rest and a drink of water at the fountain. After a couple of minutes, his stitch was almost gone so he stood up and tore off again. By the time he made it to the takeoff board thingamabob he was going . . . well . . . he was going forward.

To everyone's amazement he actually set a new St. Hall's long jump record. To no one's amazement it was the record for the **WORST** long jump in the school's history. Ben didn't actually make it into the pit. Heck, he hardly cleared the takeoff board what's-you-ma-call-it. In sheer exhaustion from his mammoth run-up, he'd tripped over (collapsed, some might say) just short of the takeoff board thingy and landed face-first on the other side of it. Well bits of him did. His nose, to be accurate.

Still, at least he didn't get any sand in his trumpet.

"Eight centimeters," called Mark Fotheringham-Smythe, as he examined the tape measure. "Bad luck, Ben."

Ben rolled to the side of the runway, hoping that broken noses didn't impact on your trumpet playing.

Mr. Snodgrass stood to the side slowly shaking his head. "Next!"

Veejay Cameron reluctantly began his run-up, mumbling under his breath the entire time. Though "run-up" is probably the wrong

wording. He ran ten paces forward and then five back. He continued doing this all the way to the pit, throwing in a few twirls along the road. Unfortunately for Veejay, he hit the board on his tenth stride forward, which meant that he had to go back five before continuing forward again.

"Thirteen centimeters," said Mark Fotheringham-Smythe. He turned to Veejay. "You would have jumped further if you hadn't been busy singing the chorus line from *Treasure Island*."

"Thank *yooo–uuuuu*," sang Veejay, who despite everything was pretty pleased with his effort. Well, he'd beaten Ben.

No sooner had Mark Fotheringham-Smythe finished measuring Veejay's "jump" than Pongo Twistleton came **BOING-BOING-BOING-ING** down the runway. He hit the takeoff board, sailed through the air like a—well, like a boy sailing through the air on a pogo stick—and landed in the sand with a sort of **THWAKA-WHAKA-WHAKA** sound. The pogo stick stuck fast in the sand, recoiled and then hurled Pongo through the air for a further

ten meters, where he landed face-first on the other side of the long jump pit.

"Er, sir," said Mark Fotheringham-Smythe. "Do I measure to the pogo stick, or where Pongo landed?" Mark scratched his impossibly blond head. "Sir? Sir?"

Unfortunately, Mr. Snodgrass couldn't hear a word Mark was saying as he was too busy banging his head against the ground.

The boys all stood around looking at each other. A couple of them wondered if they should go and get Mr. Kinkoffen, who would no doubt have a procedure about what to do in the event of a teacher banging their head against the ground.

"Okay," said Mr. Snodgrass finally. He clambered to his feet, wobbling slightly. "That's everyone. We're done here."

"Wait a minute," said Jake Chen as he rolled his wheelchair into the middle of the runway. "I want a go."

Mr. Snodgrass went back to beating his head against the ground.

"Okay, Jake," said Mark Fotheringham-

Smythe. He'd taken over the lesson for the moment because it looked as though Mr. Snodgrass was unconscious.

Jake stared down the runway, spat on his hands and rubbed them together. He didn't know what spitting on your hands did for you, but he'd seen it in a movie once and had always wanted to give it a go.

"It'll be quite hard to get this thing air-borne," said Jake to Mark Fotheringham-Smythe. "You don't have a skateboard ramp, do you?"

"Well, not on me," replied Mark, who was annoyed at himself for not dragging a ramp around with him in the event that a kid in a wheelchair wanted to have a go at the long jump. As school captain and leader of the local scout troop he should have been prepared for this situation. "How about a couple of fence palings on some bricks?"

"Yeah," replied Jake. "That'll work."

Fotheringham-Smythe dispatched a couple of boys to retrieve some fence palings and bricks from Mr. Janitor's private stash.

When they returned they positioned the bricks on the takeoff board and placed the fence palings on top, creating a sort of ramp.

With a cheery thumbs-up from Fotheringham-Smythe, Jake began his ~~run~~ wheel-up.

"Go, Jake," yelled Ben with his nose cupped in his hands.

"*Climb every mountain*," sang Veejay.

"He'll never generate enough speed," said Pongo, who was still spitting up chunks of sand from his earlier collision with the long jump pit.

But that's where they were wrong. *Very* wrong. You see, although Ben, Pongo and Veejay knew that their friend was brainy, what they didn't realize was just how brainy he actually was.

When people first saw Jake they tended to say something like, "Oh, look. That poor boy's in a wheelchair." What no one ever said was, "Oh, look. That poor boy's in a **ROCKET-POWERED WHEELCHAIR!**" which would have been more accurate.

Jake's father was a rocket scientist, and they

say that the apple doesn't fall very far from the tree. Or in this case, the rocket doesn't.

Jake was constantly sneaking into his father's lab and tinkering with wicks, candles and weapons-grade plutonium. He once tested a homemade whoopee cushion on one of his unsuspecting aunts, and the resulting explosion had demolished half the house and nearly put his aunt into orbit. Fortunately, his aunt had blamed the cherry cheesecake that his mother had made for afternoon tea. Cherries, she claimed, gave her terrible wind.

Halfway down the runway, Jake positioned his finger over a button that he'd labeled:

He'd had some trouble with his souped-up wheelchair (like his whoopee cushion) so as his finger hovered over the skull button he wasn't entirely sure *what* was going to happen, but he was pretty sure it was going to be awesome!

Jake took a deep breath and hit the button. There was a moment's silence followed by what sounded suspiciously like Krakatoa erupting (or an aunt suffering the aftereffects of way too much cherry cheesecake). Flames shot out of the back of Jake's wheelchair as it began tearing down the runway. He hit the fence palings square on and shot up the makeshift ramp.

FOREST AVENUE P.S.
20 Forest Avenue
Mississauga, ON
L5G 1K7

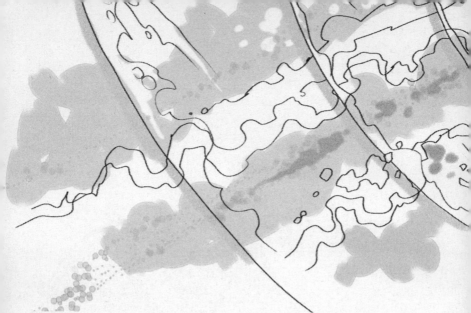

Not only did he clear the long jump pit, he cleared the school grounds and the suburb, leaving startled birds in his wake! His wheelchair flashed across the rooftops of the local houses and over the horizon. He eventually landed in the parking lot of the Reformed Church of the Flying Spaghetti Monster, where the parishioners immediately started praising him.

Meanwhile, back at St. Hall's, Jake's classmates were staring dumbstruck at his distant plume of smoke. Even Ben, who could normally talk underwater while playing his

trumpet, just stood there with his mouth hanging open.

"What, what, what's going on?" Mr. Snodgrass dragged himself gingerly to his feet. He'd been having a pleasant dream where he was in heaven and everyone played rugby 24/7 whether they wanted to or not.

"Er," said Mark Fotheringham-Smythe. He wasn't quite sure how to break the news to his teacher. "It seems, sir, that, er, Jake Chen has just broken the long jump world record. By a few kilometers, and—"

But Mr. Snodgrass was unconscious again before Mark had finished the sentence.

THE FINAL STRAW

The mortal enemies of the ninja are the samurai, phantom agents, zombies, bullies and, of course, pirates. If you ever come across a zombified pirate who is learning the art of phantom agency from a bullying samurai, he must be obliterated.

The Ninja Warrior's Handbook, Volume 27

"That's so unfair," said Ben. "Mr. Kinkoffen gave you a DT for breaking the world long jump record?"

"No," replied Jake as the four of them walked, wheeled and **BOINGED** their way over the crosswalk outside the school. "I'm getting a PE award at assembly for that. Or at least I will be once they fix up Hall's hall. Hugo Frog-Morton's spontaneous combustion blew out the wall of Hall's hall hall and hall."

"So what did you get the DT for?" asked Veejay.

"For leaving the school grounds without permission."

They came to the alleyway that led down to the station. They were running late for their train because Mr. Kinkoffen kept the entire student body back to lecture them on unauthorized spontaneous combustions, and leaving the school grounds (on rocket-powered wheelchairs or not) without permission. They were also late because they had tried to sneak up on the men in orange jackets again, but were thwarted in their efforts by the fact that the men in orange jackets had gone home.

They stared down into the dark depths of the notorious tree-lined alley and gulped in unison. St. Hall's students usually gave the alley a wide berth, even though it meant walking, wheeling and **BOINGING** an extra two kilometers out of their way to get to the station. The legendary St. Ponsonby's school bully, Crispin Staniforth, hung around the alley before and after school, scoffing, sneering, and wearing provocative haircuts. Any students

from St. Hall's who ventured down the alley were in for a hard time.

"Let's risk it," said Jake, who was feeling particularly daring having broken the school, district, zone, state, national and world long jump record, without even stretching first.

"Are you nuts?" replied Ben.

Like bullies throughout the ages, Crispin Staniforth didn't do all of the actual bullying himself. Adolf Hitler didn't invade Poland alone on a tricycle, he got armed thugs to do it for him. The notorious gangster Al Capone didn't go around threatening people with a baseball bat . . . (well, okay, he did, but that was only because he liked baseball). Likewise, Crispin Staniforth made the Nimrod twins extract money from anyone foolish enough to venture down the alley.

The Nimrod twins weren't actually twins. They weren't even brothers. But some people reckoned that they shared the same brain, because they obviously didn't have two between them. What they lacked in brains, they more than made up for in beef. To say they

were humongous is a gross (or humongous) understatement. They made Veejay look like Wee Willy Winky.

NIMROD 1

BAD GUY RATING: ☠☠☠☠

STRENGTHS: Brute force. Can crush an 800 gram can of dog food with one hand. Don't let that be your arm or your iPhone.

WEAKNESSES: Pretty butterflies. Nimrod 1 loves a pretty butterfly. Catch and release a butterfly of the silver-spotted variety and you'll have at least 5 minutes, 52 seconds to get away.

NIMROD 2

BAD GUY RATING: ☠☠☠☠

STRENGTHS: Can block narrow passages (such as Hall's hall hall) just by standing still. One should always have an alternative exit route available.

WEAKNESSES: Hot meat pies. Can detect a hot meat pie from over 200 meters away. Will not let anything get between him and a meat pie. Great decoy, especially when teamed with tomato sauce.

"Anyway, he isn't always there," argued Jake. "And he often gives the Nimrod twins the afternoon off, so they can go to their remedial breathing lessons."

"And besides," said Pongo, "we have a secret weapon." He nodded towards Jake's wheelchair.

"Riiiight," said Ben. Of course. He'd forgotten about Jake's rocket-powered turbo charger.

"Coming?" said Jake to Veejay. He rolled his wheelchair into the alley.

"Okay," said Veejay. "But if he kills me, I'm not singing to you in the afterlife."

"Can I please have that in writing?" asked Jake.

The four of them made their way cautiously down the alley. It was weird but the further they ventured into the alley the darker it became. It was as if the trees and shrubs that overlooked the alley were closing in on them.

"I say," came a voice from nowhere. "If it isn't a bunch of beastly St. Hall's rotters." Crispin Staniforth emerged from the undergrowth posing with a pipe and a copy of *The Financial Times* tucked under his arm. "What gives you

68

the temerity, nay, the impudence to venture down this squalid little alleyway?"

Crispin Staniforth was not your average bully.

"You really are the most wretched collection of utter dribbles that I've ever had the misfortune to encounter," he sneered. "I don't know whether to have you beaten senseless, or just spend several hours chortling at your effrontery."

"Effrontery?" whispered Ben to Jake. "Is that a word? I'm not sure it's a word."

"Silence, you dingbat, or I will do such things—*what they are yet I know not, but they shall be the terrors of the earth.* That's from *King Lear*, in case you were wondering," said Crispin.

"We weren't," said Jake.

That was another thing about Crispin Staniforth. Very few bullies went around quoting William Shakespeare. Very few bullies went around wearing a necktie and a monocle either. But don't let his pleasant demeanor fool you. Last year alone (last *financial* year) Crispin Staniforth had made over one hundred thousand dollars (before tax) extorting money

from students. And if the Nimrod twins weren't around to do it for him, he'd demand the money himself.

He peered out at Ben through his monocle. *"Effrontery. Shameless or impudent boldness; barefaced audacity,"* he quoted.

"Riiiiiight," said Ben.

"Okay, you little blisters," said Crispin, finally getting to the point. "Cough up your lunch money or face my unholy wrath."

"It's the afternoon," said Pongo. "We've already spent our lunch money."

Crispin chortled at this. He loved a good chortle and spent many hours practicing his chortles in front of the mirror.

"That's your problem, not mine," he said through one of his finest chortles. He slowly approached.

Pongo looked at Ben and Veejay and nodded towards Jake's wheelchair. They both instantly understood what he was getting at— time to go!

"Right," said Pongo. "Now!" The three of them leapt on Jake's wheelchair. Actually, that's not

quite right. The three of them leapt on Jake because there was no room on his chair.

"Okay, Jake," said Ben. **"HIT IT!"**

Ben tried to think of something clever as a final insult to Crispin Staniforth. In the end he settled for a loud and cheery, **"TALLY-HO, YOU ST. PONSONBY'S PEST!"**

The three of them held on tight but nothing happened . . .

"C'mon, Jake," screamed Veejay at the top of his voice, almost shattering Crispin Staniforth's monocle. "Go!"

The three of them held on tight but nothing continued to happen. The wheelchair wouldn't move.

"Come on," yelled Pongo, whose pogo stick was tucked in an uncomfortable position. "Move it!"

"Er, guys," said Jake. "I can't. I'm out of rocket fuel."

"You're kidding," said Ben.

"Nope," replied Jake. "Sorry."

Ben, Veejay and Pongo untangled themselves from Jake and his wheelchair.

"I knew we should have taken the long way," said Ben.

Crispin Staniforth was practically convulsing with chortles as he stood by and watched. "You really are the most pathetic bunch of dweebs that I have ever . . ." He trailed off. There was a lengthy silence as Crispin studied them closely through his monocle. He actually removed it and gave it a wipe to get a better look at

the four friends. He stared at Veejay's crisply ironed shirt and trousers, which still held their knife edge creases even though it was well into the afternoon. He gazed at Pongo's pants which were almost pulled up to his armpits. He gawked at Ben's knee-length socks, which he'd pulled up to, well, his knees. He also noticed that each and every shirt pocket of the foursome contained a collection of pens, and that strange boy, who insisted on singing rather than talking, had his in color-coded order.

"Oh, my word!" exclaimed Crispin Staniforth. "I've just realized who you are."

"Who are we?" said Ben.

"Why, you're **NOBODY**," replied Crispin.

"*Nobody?*" sang Veejay.

"Affirmative," said Crispin. **"YOU'RE NERDS**. In fact I would go so far as to say that you are **UBER NERDS**."

"Uber nerds?" repeated Pongo.

"That's right," continued Crispin. **"UBER NERDS. ULTRA NERDS. THE NERDIEST NERDS IN NERDTOWN."**

"So," said Ben.

"So?" replied Crispin. "I have my reputation to consider. I can't be seen to be bullying nerds. I'll be thrown out of the bullies' club. We have standards, you know. Bullying you lot would be like a lion batting wingless fruit flies."

"There's a bullies' club?" asked Jake. "And you have rules?"

"Of course we have rules! There's a code we must respect!"

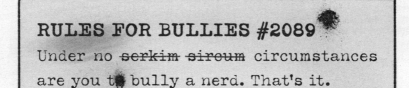

RULES FOR BULLIES #2089
Under no ~~serkim~~ ~~sircum~~ circumstances are you to bully a nerd. That's it.

"Quick!" continued Crispin. "Get out, go. Scram." Crispin Staniforth disappeared back into the undergrowth as quickly as he'd emerged.

"Did you see that?" said Ben to Jake. "He didn't even tip his hat at us."

The four friends slumped along to the other side of the alley towards the train station.

Veejay had no desire to sing anything. Ben couldn't even manage to blow a raspberry on his trumpet. Although it was quite difficult, Jake managed to make his wheelchair appear as though it was trudging. Even the spring had gone out of Pongo's pogo stick, so he dragged it along behind them.

They eventually made it to the end of the alley, turned back and stared into its depths. In the distance they could just hear Crispin Staniforth declare, "I say. If it isn't a bunch of beastly St. Hall's rotters."

A few minutes later several younger St. Hall's students came tearing down the alley in a highly animated fashion. They swept past Ben, Jake, Pongo and Veejay as if they didn't exist.

"Can you believe it?" said one of them in an excited voice. "We just got bullied by Crispin Staniforth! *The* Crispin Staniforth!"

"He took my lunch money for this week *and* the next!" said another.

"I can't wait to get onto Facebook and tell everyone," said a third who was so thrilled he was practically bursting.

"How come they got bullied, and we didn't?" said Ben, looking at his friends.

"That's not fair," agreed Pongo.

"I've had enough," said Jake. "That's the final straw." He pointed his wheelchair to the station and rolled off into the afternoon. His three friends loped along behind him.

THE NINJAS ARE BORN

The record for ninja concealment is currently held by Shinto Hijakairi. Rather than accompanying his wife on a shopping trip, Ninja Hijakairi vanished into the woods behind his house. He remains there some 47 years later. His wife is still at the shops.

The Ninja Warrior's Handbook, Volume 27

The meeting took place in Jake's tree house. Jake didn't let a little thing like being in a wheelchair stop him from having a tree house. Heck, Jake didn't let a little thing like being in a wheelchair stop him from doing anything. Okay, his legs didn't work. But his arms did. And because he used them to get around, he was as strong as an ox. He could zip up the old rope ladder like a monkey.

Jake usually had to wait for everyone else at the top as they stumbled clumsily up the ladder. This time he was forced to wait longer

than usual because Veejay chickened out halfway up and couldn't be coaxed either up or down. In the end they had to blindfold him and sing the national anthem before he would budge.

Jake, Ben and Pongo also had to sweep the tree house for spiders because Veejay was terrified of them. Veejay, as Jake was slowly beginning to realize, was a complex guy. Apart from acrophobia (fear of heights) and arachnophobia (fear of spiders), Veejay also suffered from:

Agrizoophobia fear of wild animals

Alektorophobia fear of chickens

Agyiophobia fear of crossing the street

Apeirophobia fear of infinity

Arachibutyrophobia fear of peanut butter sticking to the roof of the mouth

Bogyphobia fear of the bogeyman

Chiroptophobia fear of bats

Entomophobia fear of insects

Geniophobia fear of chins. *Note: Veejay has a note from his mother stating that he's not allowed to be taught by Mrs. Attenborough because of her abundance of chins*

Hippopotomonstrosesquipedaliophobia fear of long words. *Note: No one believes Veejay suffers from hippopotomonstrosesquipe- daliophobia, he just likes to tell people that he does*

Katsaridaphobia fear of cockroaches

Omphalophobia fear of belly buttons

Pteronophobia fear of being tickled by someone with a feather

Fearophobia fear of fear

Fearofearophobia fear of fearophobia

Veejayophobia fear of being himself

Anti-Veejayophobia fear of being someone else

Pegapronophobia fear of being seen in public wearing nothing but his mother's clothesline peg apron

Ben felt it must have been hard work being Veejay. It was certainly hard work being his friend. Pongo now carried a feather with him everywhere.

Finally the four of them were ready.

"Unless you have a fear of meetings," said Ben.

"No, why?" said Veejay nervously, who also lived in mortal fear of creeks and the fear that gravity might suddenly stop working or the sun might inexplicably go out. "That would be silly."

"Riiight," said Ben.

"Right," said Pongo. "So what's up, Jake?" he asked.

"This," said Jake. "I'm tired of living like this."

"What?" said Ben. "Tired of being in a wheelchair?"

"No," replied Jake. "I'm tired of being a nerd."

"What do you mean?" said Ben. "What's wrong with being a nerd?"

Jake took a deep breath. "We get picked last for sports. Girls totally ignore us. Everyone laughs at us. People do rabbit ears behind

Jake Yr K

Jake Yr 3

Jake Yr 6

our heads in every single photo we've ever had taken."

"But that's always happened," said Pongo. "Ever since a piece of primordial sludge stuck a couple of primitive pens in its shirt pocket, nerds have been treated like lesser life forms."

"Yeah," agreed Ben. "It's as if it's cool to be a moron."

"My mother always says it's better to have brains than brawn," said Veejay.

"Well I've had it!" said Jake. "When Crispin Staniforth refused to bully us—that was the final straw. I can take being called **FOUR EYES, EGGHEAD, HUMAN CALCULATOR, GEEK, NERD, DRIP** and **WEED** . . . but to be considered **TOO PATHETIC TO BULLY AND EXTORT MONEY OUT OF, WELL SOMETHING HAS TO BE DONE!** It's time we took a stand."

Veejay put down the *Batman* comic book that he was reading. "What?" he said. "Aren't you going to be a nerd anymore?"

"Jake's right. I don't think we have a choice," said Ben.

"It's time we had some respect," continued Jake. "Maybe we should join a gang."

Ben burst out laughing. "Who'd let us join their gang?"

"Okay then," said Jake. "Let's form our own." "What are we going to do?" said Ben. "Hold people up in alleyways and explain scientific theories to them?"

Theorists maintain that time travel is possible at the subatomic particle level. So there.

"I've got it," said Ben. "We could become superheroes."

"Superheroes?" said Veejay.

"Superheroes aren't nerds," said Jake.

"I beg to differ," said Ben, who thought there was nothing wrong with saying things like *I beg to differ*. "Think about it. Superman was a four-eyed reporter. Batman was like a rich dude with a butler and a boy friend called Robin."

"Boyfriend?" repeated Jake.

"No," replied Ben. "Boy friend. Two words. And Spiderman was . . . was a . . . what was Spiderman?"

"He was a guy who was bitten by a spider," said Pongo.

"I don't want to be a superhero," said Veejay. "I'm not going around with my undies on the outside of my clothes. My mom would never let me leave the house looking like that, unless it was for a religious festival or something."

"Good point," said Jake. "There's also the small matter of us not having any superpowers."

"Yes, well, that's where my plan falls down a bit," said Ben.

"Hardly anyone notices that we're even there half the time," said Jake. "It's like we're invisible. We have to use our brains and find a way of using that to our advantage."

"You're right, people don't notice us. But how are we supposed to use that?" asked Ben. "By entering the world hide 'n' seek championships or something?"

"They have that?" said Veejay.

"What's up, Pongo?" said Ben. Pongo had been staring at the same spot on the tree house wall for about ten minutes. Veejay hoped that he hadn't seen a spider.

"I think I might have it," said Pongo. "Yes! Invisible! That's it! We could become . . ." He paused for effect. "We could become . . . **NINJAS!**"

The other three looked at Pongo as if he was mad. Okay, he was definitely mad, but the question was just how mad was he?

"Ninjas are masters of disguise and sneaking around," said Pongo. "There could be twenty of them hiding in this tree house right now and we'd never know."

"Ninjas?" said Jake. "How on earth could four of the nerdiest nerds in the whole of nerd-dom become ninjas? We'd need help!"

"My dad," replied Pongo.

"Your dad's a ninja?" asked Ben.

"No," said Pongo. "But he has this ultimate ninja DVD we can watch."

8

THE mysterious EXPLODING ISLAND

Whenever at the beach, a ninja should hide his wallet and other valuables in his shoe before going for a dip. A criminal mastermind would never think of looking there.

The Ninja Warrior's Handbook, Volume 27

So far the DVD hadn't made a lot of sense. Actually it wasn't even a DVD, it was an ancient video. It may have even been pre-video. What was that? A cave painting? Anyway, in the episode they were watching, a couple of ninjas had planted a bomb on a deserted island. It wasn't clear why they went around doing that, other than perhaps they liked planting bombs on deserted islands. And now, while their colleagues waited safely offshore in a rowboat, two Phantom Agents were trying to disarm the bomb. It wasn't clear

why they went around disarming bombs on deserted islands other than perhaps they liked disarming bombs on deserted islands.

Suddenly there was an almighty explosion. (Well of course it was suddenly. You wouldn't say: *Gradually there was an almighty explosion.*) To Ben it looked like a nuclear bomb going off, which seemed a bit excessive just to get rid of a couple of Phantom Agents.

For a show about ninjas, they didn't get much screen time. In fact for the entire episode they only briefly glimpsed one ninja. He jumped out from behind a rock, hurled a couple of sharpened key-rings at the Phantom Agents, mumbled something under his breath, and then to everyone's surprise, leapt about 30 meters backwards into a tree and disappeared. They only knew that the bomb had been planted by ninjas because one of the Phantom Agents said, "Oh, look. There's the bomb that has been planted by the ninjas. We had better disarm it." This was about a millisecond before the thing exploded and seriously messed up their afternoon.

The episode ended when the other Phantom Agents rowed ashore to see how their friends had fared in the explosion. When they arrived at the blast site, all the Phantom Agents found were a couple of pairs of boots with smoke billowing out of them. The Phantom Agents immediately knew that their friends were either dead, or off somewhere writing a letter to the boot manufacturer praising them on the quality and durability of their boots.

"What on earth was all that about?" said Jake when the video had finished.

"I have no idea," said Veejay, scratching his head.

"And what was the deal with that ninja throwing those key-rings at the Phantom Agent dudes?" said Ben.

"They weren't key-rings," said Pongo. "They were shurikens."

"What are shurikens?" asked Veejay.

"Kind of like really sharp—"

"Key-rings," finished Jake and Ben together.

"And what was with the ninjas?" asked Ben. "We only saw one. Were the others on strike or something?"

"No," said Pongo. He had become a sort of ninja spokesperson. "Like I said before, ninjas are masters of disguise and camouflage. For all we know there could have been 300 of them hiding out in that forest."

"Or one," said Veejay.

While Mrs. Twistleton made the boys lunch (colored popcorn and fairy bread) Veejay flicked through *The Ninja Warrior's Handbook*, Volume 27, that also belonged to Pongo's father. Either Mr. Twistleton was a secret ninja assassin, or he was bored out of his mind with his work as an accountant for the country's

fourth leading toilet paper manufacturer and yearned to be a secret ninja assassin.

After lunch the four friends watched a couple more episodes of the old video. The ninjas went around blowing up bridges, derailing trains, kidnapping people and hurling them into rivers. They also spent a lot of time throwing their specially sharpened key-rings (shurikens, insisted Pongo) at people and leaping backwards into trees and tall buildings.

Ben felt that if he could leap backwards like that, he wouldn't bother with hurling-people-into-rivers. He'd enter the Olympic Games high jump competition.

Even if they did do some weird things, Jake, Ben, Pongo and even Veejay thought that the ninjas were pretty cool.

"So, what next?" asked Jake when Pongo turned off the last episode. "We'll need some sort of physical ninja training."

"Maybe we could enroll at a ninja school," suggested Pongo.

"Count me out," said Veejay, who was not allowed to cross the road. Any road.

90

"Training DVD?" suggested Ben. "There's got to be one available online. You can buy anything online. My grandmother bought a DVD about training a three-legged poodle."

"Your grandmother's poodle only has three legs?" asked Jake.

"No," said Ben. "But the DVD about training *four*-legged poodles was too expensive."

"What about Mr. Lee in Emu Crescent?" said Pongo, getting back to the point. "Maybe we could get *him* to teach us."

"Is Mr. Lee a ninja?" whispered Veejay.

"He must be," said Pongo. "He's very light on his feet, quiet and he almost always wears black."

"That's because his wife died," said Jake.

"Maybe his wife died *and* he's a ninja," suggested Ben.

The four of them agreed that it was worth a shot. Twenty minutes later and the four of them were tip-toeing (or in Jake's case, tip-wheeling, and Pongo's tip-**BOINGING**) up Mr. Lee's driveway.

THE TRAINING BEGINS

When confronted by a wild bear a ninja must remember this: If it's a brown bear run away. If it's a grizzly bear play dead. Or is it the other way round?

The Ninja Warrior's Handbook, Volume 27

They had to ring the doorbell about 20 times before Mr. Lee answered it. When he finally opened the door he had a calm, almost serene, expression on his face, as if his mind was somewhere else.

"Sorry, Mr. Lee," said Pongo. "Were you meditating?"

"No," replied Mr. Lee. "Watching beach volleyball in high definition."

"Riiiight," said Ben.

"Can you please teach us how to be ninjas?" said Jake, getting down to business.

"Ninjas?" said Mr. Lee. "What's this about ninjas?"

"We were sort of wondering if you would er . . ." Veejay trailed off.

"If I would *er*?" said Mr. Lee. "Wait a minute. You do odd jobs for Mr. Lee?"

The four friends looked at each other and nodded. Mr. Lee would teach them how to be ninjas and in return they would do odd jobs for him! That seemed like a fair trade!

Ten minutes later Jake was washing Mr. Lee's car, Pongo was hanging clothes on the line, Ben was mowing the lawn, and Veejay was tending to the flower beds.

"This is perfect," said Pongo. "It's just like one of those movies where the wise old teacher makes his students do boring jobs over and over and over again, and then just when they start to suspect that they're being ripped off and are going to quit, he shows them what they've learned."

"What do you mean?" said Ben as he pushed and pulled the ancient, motor-less lawnmower back and forth across the grass.

93

"Think about it," said Pongo with a smile. "You're exercising your leg muscles on that ancient lawnmower. Jake's learning how to block punches by polishing the car."

"Actually," said Jake, "I just hosed off the dirt."

Pongo ignored him. "I'm building up my shoulders by hanging out the washing."

Ben nodded. Maybe there *was* something to this.

"What about me?" said Veejay, looking over at them with his pruning sheers.

The three of them looked at Veejay and his floral gardening gloves.

"Well you're..." Pongo trailed off and scratched his head. "Maybe you're . . ."

"He's just pruning roses," said Jake. There was no other way of looking at it.

When the boys had finished their chores they went back around the front and knocked on Mr. Lee's door. There was no answer. They tried again. Nothing. They tried a third time. Still nothing.

Eventually Pongo gently pushed the door open. The four of them stepped cautiously into Mr. Lee's house.

Pongo called out. "Mr. Lee?"

Ben echoed him. "Mr. Lee?"

Jake also chimed in. "Mr. Lee?"

"Come out, come out wherever you are," sang Veejay.

"We're not playing hide 'n' seek," snapped Jake.

"No, but maybe Veejay's right." Suddenly Pongo became very animated. "This is our first lesson. Mr. Lee's hiding somewhere and we have to find him. Let's split up!"

"Hang on a cotton-picking minute," complained Veejay, who saw nothing wrong with saying things like cotton-picking minute. "No way I'm agreeing to splitting up. Every movie I've ever seen where the characters decide to split up to get away from the ax murderer, it's always someone like *me* who gets killed first."

"Mr. Lee isn't trying to kill us," said Pongo. "He's just trying to teach us the arts of camouflage and disguise."

"Still not splitting up," said Veejay.

"Okay," said Ben, "you stay there and *we'll* split up."

"Don't forget," said Pongo, ignoring Veejay, who looked like he was about to throw a major tantrum, "he could be anywhere. Under the kitchen sink. Up in the loft. In the toilet bowl."

"In the silverware drawer?" suggested Jake sarcastically.

"Exactly," said Pongo, and Jake rolled his eyes.

Just as they were about to head off in search of him, Mr. Lee walked in through the front door with his ancient beagle.

"Ah," said Mr. Lee. "You finished jobs?"

"Yes," said Pongo. "We thought you were in camouflage."

"Not camouflage," said Mr. Lee. "Taking Mao Zedong for walkies."

"Mao Zedong?" said Veejay. "Wasn't he the great leader of the Chinese revolution?"

"Yes," agreed Mr. Lee. "Also pet pooch."

"So when are you going to teach us to become ninjas?" asked Pongo, practically bursting with enthusiasm.

"What's all this about ninjas?" asked Mr. Lee. He pulled out his wallet and handed the boys a dollar each.

The four friends looked at each other.

"What's this for?" asked Jake.

"For jobs," said Mr. Lee. "Very grateful."

"What about teaching us to be ninjas?" Pongo was practically begging now.

Mr. Lee scratched his head. "Ninja Japanese," he said. "I'm Chinese. Chinese speciality is kung fu."

"Great," said Pongo. "You could teach us kung fu then!"

"Well, I could . . ." said Mr. Lee, "if I knew kung fu."

"Then why did you make us do all those odd jobs?" asked Veejay, who'd almost been pricked to death by the rose bushes.

"I thought you were boy scouts," said Mr. Lee. "Do odd jobs to help elderly neighbor."

"Riiight," said Ben.

"Couldn't you at least tell us something wise then?" asked Pongo.

Mr. Lee scratched his head and smiled. "Okay. How about this? Man who speak with forked tongue been hiding in silverware drawer again."

Pongo turned to the others. "See! I told you ninjas could hide in silverware drawers."

"He's not a ninja!" reminded Jake.

"Anything else?" pleaded Pongo. He knew they needed something—anything—to help face Crispin Staniforth again.

"Remember," said Mr. Lee as he ushered the boys towards his door. "Everything we do, we do first in mind. If you believe you are a ninja, then you are a ninja."

REVENGE OF THE NINJAS

To determine whether a fence is electrified
or not, a ninja is strongly advised NOT to
pee against it.

The Ninja Warrior's Handbook, Volume 27

The ~~four~~ three assassins lurked silently in the shadows waiting to snare their prey. They checked their swords and shurikens again, even though they'd already checked and rechecked them before they'd left their secret hideout.

There should have been a fourth ninja with them, but he'd gone missing in mysterious circumstances. Maybe he'd been lost on the way to the mission. Attacked by vampires. Sucked up by a UFO. Or maybe he'd chickened out because he wasn't allowed to cross the road.

"Whoever heard of a ninja not being allowed to cross the road?" said Jake.

"But I'd worked out a route where he didn't have to actually cross any roads," said Ben, "so I don't know what's happened to him."

"Veejay would only give away our hiding spot anyway," continued Jake. "Veejay would be singing, 'I've got a Lovely Bunch of Coconuts' or something. Kind of makes it hard to sneak up on anyone."

"Ssshhh!" hissed Ben like a cornered snake. "He's there, I can hear him."

"Who?" said Pongo. "Veejay?"

"No," whispered Ben. "Crispin Staniforth! I can hear him rummaging around in the undergrowth reading *The Financial Times*."

There was a long pause.

"What the?" said Jake eventually. "How can you hear him reading *The Financial Times*?"

"Well I can hear the paper rustling when he turns the page," said Ben. "And as he reads *The Financial Times* I simply put two and two together."

Pongo and Jake stared at Ben.

Ben looked back at them. "That's the sort of stuff that ninjas do," he said.

Jake and Pongo looked at each other. It was funny seeing Ben without his trumpet. They were impressed. Good old Ben was turning out to be a pretty good ninja.

Fortunately, from what Ben could gather, it appeared as though the Nimrod twins weren't with Crispin again. They had heard a rumor that the Nimrods had joined the army and were being trained as tanks.

"This ski mask is really itchy," complained Jake, scratching at his neck.

"Mine too," agreed Ben.

"Will you two stop whining!" hissed Pongo. "In all that training we did in front of the TV, did you ever see a ninja complaining about his ski mask being itchy?"

"They were probably more highly trained than we are," said Jake.

"Probably had better ski masks too," said Ben.

"Yeah," continued Jake. "We just took Mr. Lee's advice to believe we're ninjas. We don't actually have a clue what we're doing."

"Yes we do," sulked Pongo. "Or we just have to *believe* we do."

"I can see a potential flaw in that technique," said Ben.

"You just have to *believe* that you can't see any flaws," argued Pongo.

"Ssshhh!" hissed Ben. "Someone's coming. And they're kids."

"Okay," said Pongo. "Let's go rescue them."

"Wait," said Jake. "You've got to give me time to go around."

In order to stay out of sight in the shadows, the Nerdy Ninjas had lain in wait in the vacant block of land that adjoins the alley. So now they had to wait for Jake to negotiate his wheelchair out of the vacant block and back down the other side of the alley to where Crispin Staniforth did his bullying.

Fortunately for the Nerdy Ninjas, Jake was as strong as a rhino and made it out of the vacant block in next to no time. *Unfortunately* for the Nerdy Ninjas, one of Jake's wheels was badly in need of oiling. Pongo and Ben could hear him **SQUEAK, SQUEAK,**

SQUEAKING down the alley like a plague of mice.

But Crispin Staniforth hadn't heard Jake as he was busy with his first bullying of the day. "I say. If it isn't a bunch of beastly St. Hall's rotters," he scoffed. "You really are the most wretched collection of utter dribbles that I've ever had the misfortune to encounter."

At the sound of his voice, Pongo and Ben leapt over the fence and into action.

Or rather, that's what they'd *planned* on doing.

In reality, Pongo's pogo stick malfunctioned **mid-BOING**, sending him hurtling backwards into a tree. Ben just wasn't very good at climbing fences, so the two of them ended up hammering loose a couple of fence palings with Pongo's pogo stick so that they could squeeze their way through.

As they were busy battering down the fence, Jake was **SQUEAKING** up behind Crispin Staniforth.

At the sound of the fence collapsing, both bully and bullied leapt back in shock. Jake looked over at Pongo and Ben and shook his head. If they could have read his thought bubble at that moment, it would have said something like, "You've got to be kidding me!"

"SURPRISE!" yelled Ben, unsheathing his sword and brandishing it at Crispin Staniforth.

"Ninjas don't yell out 'Surprise'!" Pongo hissed to Ben.

"No?" said Ben. "What do they say?"

"Nothing!" said Pongo.

"Well it's probably a bit late for that," said Ben. He turned to Crispin Staniforth. "Do you mind if we start over?"

Jake's eyes rolled so far back in his head that they almost went all the way around.

Crispin Staniforth examined the ~~four~~ three ninjas through his monocle.

"I say there, ninjas," he said. "What the Dickens is all this about? I'm busy bullying. What do you want?"

Pongo unsheathed his sword. "Vengeance," he said. Then he turned to the two young, bullied St. Hall's students. "Go," he said. "Run! You're free! And tell everyone that **YOU HAVE BEEN RESCUED BY THE *NERDY NINJAS!*"**

"But, wait," said one of the young boys. "Crispin Staniforth hasn't finished bullying us yet. That's not fair!"

"Just go," muttered Ben. "Please."

The two young St. Hall's students trudged off down the alley mumbling stuff about life not being fair and ninjas being stupid.

When the boys were out of sight, Jake also unsheathed his sword.

"Why are you here?" Crispin persisted.

"We told you," said Pongo. "Vengeance."

"Vengeance," said Crispin. "Why? What did I ever do to you?"

"What did you do to us?" mimicked Pongo. "You bullied us last time we came down this alley!"

There was a moment's silence.

"Actually," said Ben. "That's not quite true. He *didn't* bully us, remember?"

"Right," said Pongo, recalling how Crispin had refused to bully them because of their sheer nerdiness. "Er . . ." he began. "We don't know why we're here then."

Pongo scratched his head.

"Yes we do," said Jake. "We're here to teach him a lesson."

Crispin Staniforth gulped again. "A lesson in what?"

There was a long pause.

Pongo looked around at his fellow ninjas. "Anyone?"

Eventually Ben broke the silence. "We're going to teach you a lesson in *something*!"

That was good enough for Pongo. "Okay, ninjas," he said. "Get him!"

Jake took out a shuriken and hurled it at Crispin Staniforth. It smacked into the side of his head.

"OUCH!" yelped Crispin. "That really stung!"

Because the Nerdy Ninjas didn't really want to hurt anyone too badly, nor did they particularly want to go to jail, they decided to forget razor-sharp shurikens, and instead started throwing squash balls. Luckily Ben's father was an A-grade squash player and they were able to raid his private stash. Ben had selected a variety and spray-painted them silver to make them appear more threatening and shuriken-like.

"OUCH! OOOOCH! EEEEK!" yelped Crispin like a cat on a cactus.

"Let that be a lesson to you," said Pongo.

"A lesson in what?" shouted Crispin, dodging the silver squash balls as best he could.

"We don't know!" replied Pongo.

The Nerdy Ninjas then set about Crispin with their swords, which were rolled up newspapers.

Crispin Staniforth tried to fight back by rolling up his copy of *The Financial Times* but he really didn't stand a chance. It wasn't that his attackers believed they were ninjas at that moment, but more to do with the fact that they were using the *Sydney Morning Herald* weekend edition, which was about as thick and as heavy as a baseball bat!

"OUCH! OOOOCH! EEEEK!" yelped Crispin as the Nerdy Ninjas finally whacked and thwacked *The Financial Times* out of his hands. Crispin Staniforth had such an awesome reputation as a bully that no one had ever bothered fighting back before. And because he had no practice, he didn't know how to fight. Chortle, yes. Fight, no. And it was around this time that he began to regret allowing the Nimrod twins to leave and join the army. And

it was around this time that he also began to regret sending the "Nerdy Ninjas" on their way for being *too nerdy* last encounter. He certainly wouldn't forget them now!

In the end he collapsed on the ground, begging for mercy and crying for his mommy.

"And don't do it again!" sneered Pongo.

"Don't do what?" whimpered Crispin.

"Um, um . . . whatever!" said Jake.

The Nerdy Ninjas watched as Crispin Staniforth clambered to his feet and tore off down the alley, across the road (pausing to walk briskly over the crosswalk), and then over to the train station.

The boys then sheathed their swords.

"Ninjas one, bullies nil," said Pongo. "Let's go back to the secret hideout and debrief."

"Wait a sec," said Ben. "Can you help me pick up the shurikens? Dad's got a big game tonight."

11

THE really REALLY BAD GUYS

A ninja's garments should always be black,
unless he finds himself in a snowstorm, then white
is preferred. If a ninja is hiding among a herd of
zebras, then a combination of the two is advised.

The Ninja Warrior's Handbook, Volume 27

The ~~four~~ three assassins returned to their secret hideout where they feasted on milk and cookies. Pongo complained to his mom that ninjas didn't go for milk and cookies, but as he didn't really have any idea what ninjas scoffed down after a mission, he decided it was okay for now.

Jake's mother took the empty tray in one hand and abseiled back down to the ground like a . . . well, like a ninja.

"Cool," said Ben as he watched Jake's mother hit the ground and drop into a sort of

alert
crouch
position.
"How did she
learn to do that?"
Jake shrugged. "She
used to be in the Chinese
special forces."

"She did not," said
Pongo.

"Okay then," said Jake.
"She used to be a spy."

"She did not," said
Pongo.

"Well then, she used to
be an abseiling and rock-
climbing instructor in Hong
Kong," said Jake.

"Really?" said Ben before
Pongo had the chance to argue.

"Actually," continued Jake,
"*one* of those is true."

Ben's eyes widened. Even
Pongo appeared stunned.

"Really," said Pongo. "Which one?"

"We don't know," said Jake. "She won't tell us."

As they were talking, they could hear something struggling up the rope ladder. Whatever it was didn't sound very graceful. It was either an asthmatic hippo that had learned how to whine in English, or else Veejay had finally turned up.

Eventually it hauled itself into the tree house and sat panting in the corner.

"Sorry I'm late," gasped the thing that wasn't an asthmatic hippo.

Jake, Ben and Pongo stared at Veejay. His clothes were so bright they were practically glowing.

"What are you wearing?" said Ben, shielding his eyes.

Veejay brushed a speck of dirt from his pants. "My ninja gear."

"But it's all white," said Pongo.

"Oh, duh," snapped Veejay. "I couldn't find any black stuff so I wore my cricket clothes."

"But you don't play cricket," said Jake.

"I know," replied Veejay. "That's why they're so clean."

Jake shook his head. "Did the weather channel forecast a blizzard?"

"Well, no, but . . ."

"It's thirty-five degrees outside already," said Ben. "And it's only ten o'clock. Not much chance of a snowstorm for you to go creeping around in."

"Our enemies will see us coming from a kilometer away if you wear that on a mission," said Pongo.

"Maybe we should just attack cricket teams," suggested Jake.

Veejay put his head in his hands. He looked like he was about to cry.

"That's okay," said Pongo, trying now to comfort his friend. "We'll only go on missions at night. The pitch black will tone down your cricket whites."

"Can't," sniffed Veejay. "I'm not allowed out of the house after seven."

"Then we'll stick with the cricket teams," said Jake.

"Or maybe we could dye his clothes black with some shoe polish," suggested Ben.

Everyone agreed that that was the best plan. Ben was coming up with all the ideas. The way things were going, Pongo might have to hand over the reins of ninja chief to Ben.

When they'd finished discussing Veejay's ~~cricket~~ ninja gear, Pongo lapsed into the tale of their first mission and how they'd sorted out Crispin Staniforth. They were confident that Crispin wouldn't do it again; or else he *would* do it again if that's what they wanted. They just weren't sure.

Jake noticed that Pongo deliberately left out certain details from his recount such as Pongo's pogo stick malfunctioning and Ben not being able to climb the fence, or Jake's wheelchair **SQUEAK, SQUEAK, SQUEAKING** down the alley, or Pongo and Ben demolishing half the fence to get into the alley. But the story made Veejay smile. He was pleased that the Nerdy Ninjas' first mission had been a huge success, even if he hadn't been there to help.

"So what happened?" said Ben. "Why are you so late?"

"I was having a milkshake with Mother at the cafe in the village," said Veejay. "She wanted to talk about university."

"University?" said Pongo. "But you're in Year Six."

"I know that," replied Veejay. "But she gets the exam papers from the university and makes me take them."

"How'd you do?" asked Ben.

"Apparently I've just qualified for my Master's degree in Mathematics."

"It's a shame you didn't turn up earlier," said Ben. "You could have rolled up your exam papers and harrangued Crispin with them."

"Forget Crispin Staniforth," said Veejay. "We're going on a real mission. A mission to save the school . . ."

A heavy silence settled over the secret hideout. Everyone stared at Veejay. This was eventually shattered when Ben had a flashback to Pongo's pogo stick malfunctioning and sending him hurtling backwards into that

tree. Unfortunately, he happened to have his flashback just as he'd gulped down a large mouthful of milk. After a brief moment where he appeared to be choking to death, the milk, along with several pieces of soggy cookie and chocolate chips, erupted out of his nose in a shower of liquid gunk.

"Er, gross!" yelped Pongo, Jake and Veejay as they leapt out of the firing line.

After Ben had mopped up the floor, Veejay told them about what had happened at the cafe. When Veejay's mother had left to go to the hospital where she worked as a surgeon, Veejay had stayed behind to finish his third milkshake. As he was slurping up the remnants he'd overheard three guys, three bad guys, three really bad guys, three really *really* bad guys talking about how they were going to **BLOW UP ST. HALL'S**.

"Blow up St. Hall's? Why?" asked Ben.

"I don't know," replied Veejay. "They didn't say."

"Well what did they look like?" asked Ben.

"Bad," said Veejay.

"Bad?" said Pongo.

"Really bad," continued Veejay. "Really *really* bad."

"That's it?" said Ben. "We can't go to the police and tell them to be on the lookout for some really *really* bad guys."

"We don't need the police," said Pongo. "This is *our* school and we're ninjas."

"Or at least we believe we are," said Jake.

"It was those three guys who've been hanging around the school in those orange jackets," said Veejay.

"How do you know?" asked Jake.

"Because," said Veejay, "they were wearing those orange jackets."

Jake sighed. "I knew they were up to no good. That wheelbarrow was probably filled with dynamite. So when are they going to blow up the school?"

"Tomorrow," replied Veejay. "Before lunch."

"Do you mean they've made lunch plans for after they blow up the school?" asked Jake.

"Yeah," replied Veejay. "They're going to that sushi place next to Larry's Lawnmowers, for the Saturday Special."

"Sushi? There's something fishy about all of this," said Pongo as the four ninjas got themselves ready for their next mission.

In the morning, the Nerdy Ninjas ran flat out towards the school in a single file with Jake setting the pace in his wheelchair. The Phantom Agents had run this way in their early missions and the four boys thought it looked way cool.

Jake was able to zoom ahead at the front of the file by releasing his brakes and freewheeling down the hills, and Veejay wasn't very fit so he kind of lagged along behind complaining. So by the time they were about halfway to school, their single file was spread out over about four kilometers. When Veejay eventually caught up, he was panting like an overloaded steam train.

"Finally," snapped Pongo at Veejay when he wheezed up to them. "We've been waiting ages. Where've you been?"

"I stopped off for some supplies in the village." Veejay opened his shopping bag and sniffed the contents. "Doughnut, anyone?"

"Ninjas don't eat doughnuts before a mission!" snapped Pongo.

"Who says?" said Ben.

"Did you see any of those ninjas climbing that high-voltage power stanchion chowing down on Krispy Kremes?" said Pongo.

"They could have had some before they started climbing," said Veejay. "For energy and that. So who wants one?"

"Me," said Ben.

"Me too," said Jake.

"You guys are the worst ninjas in the world," sneered Pongo.

"Maybe you're right," said Jake. His face was so stuffed with jam and cream that his cheeks bulged like those of a startled puffer fish. "But at least we're not the hungriest!"

"There they are," spurted Veejay, pointing over towards Brandon House and showering his fellow ninjas with the remnants of a cinnamon doughnut. "They're the three really *really* bad guys I saw in the cafe."

"But there's *four* of them," said Ben. "Are you sure that's them?"

"Yep," said Veejay. "That's definitely them. They're still wearing those orange jackets." They could see now that the men's jackets were so bright that they would probably glow in the dark. A bit like Veejay's ninja gear.

"So who's the guy in the suit?" said Pongo.

"How should I know?" said Veejay.

"Maybe he's the boss," said Ben.

"He sure is bald," said Jake. "You could skim rocks off his head."

"What are they doing over at Brandon House?" said Ben.

"That's where they said they were going to start," said Veejay. "They said they were going to demolish Brandon House and then 'take care' of the rest of the school."

The four ninjas watched as the men lurked in a sinister fashion around the entrance to Brandon House.

Brandon House had been built just after the First World War. It was named in honor of a former St. Hall's student, Lieutenant Colonel Sir Hubert Brandon, who had fought on the Western Front and had been awarded medals

for outstanding gallantry and extreme silliness. Having dragged several of his men to safety under a vicious enemy bombardment, the Lieutenant Colonel had stormed over to the German trenches, carrying nothing more than a riding crop and said, "I say there, chaps. Do you mind giving the dastardly shelling a bit of a rest for a spell? We're trying to have a jolly old game of cricket over here." The German soldiers were so stunned at Lieutenant Colonel Brandon's effrontery, that they'd obeyed his request. Or at least they had once they'd shot him 47 times and blown him up twice.

Brandon House was a relic from the past, as was Sir Hubert Brandon himself. Currently 117 years old, Sir Hubert Brandon is widely regarded as the oldest (and maddest) person on the planet.

The Nerdy Ninjas refused to let any harm come to their school—even if it was only the weekend and there were no other kids around. They'd do whatever it took to stop the really *really* bad guys.

They quickly discussed their plans. First

they were going to approach the really *really* bad guys in single file, overpower them and tie them up.

No they weren't!

They were going to sneak up on them from the flanks, overpower them and tie them up.

No they weren't!

They were going to charge towards them in a line, overpower them and tie them up.

No they weren't!

They were going to dart from the trees, roll behind the dumpster, leap out and start throwing shurikens at them (or squash balls, as most people call them), overpower them and tie them up.

Well at least they agreed on the tying-them-up bit.

Unable to come to a compromise, the Nerdy Ninjas agreed to attack the really *really* bad guys in their own preferred way.

"LET'S DO IT!" shouted Ben. "Oops, let's do it," he whispered with a shrug.

Jake ran (or rather wheeled) towards them. Veejay sneaked up towards them from the

flanks, darting behind things in his glow-in-the-dark ~~cricket~~ ninja gear. Pongo ran charging towards them in a line (on his own). And Ben rolled out from behind a tree, raced over towards the dumpster, gathered himself, leapt out from behind it with a loud **"SURPRISE!"** and started throwing shurikens (a selection of the firmest squash balls) at the bad guys.

Fortunately, the four of them somehow managed to arrive at the same time and it caught the really *really* bad guys by surprise. They were able to achieve this because Pongo's pogo stick was in for its **50,000-BOING** service, Jake had put some oil on his **SQUEAKY** wheel, they'd thrown dirt all over Veejay's glow-in-the-dark ~~cricket~~ ninja gear so it was a little less luminous now, and Jake had hidden Ben's trumpet so that he couldn't blow the cavalry charge as he ran towards them.

The really, *really* bad guys collapsed under the heavy barrage of squash balls and rolled up newspapers and while they were on the ground the four ninjas quickly tied them up.

"Ninjas don't yell out 'Surprise,'" reminded

Pongo when they had subdued the really *really* bad guys.

"Sorry," said Ben. "I got carried away again."

"What's going on here?" said the bald guy in the suit who looked vaguely familiar. "What in the world do you think you're doing?"

"Well might we ask you?" said Pongo who'd heard that line in a movie once and had wanted to try it out. Not that he knew what it meant. Still, it sounded good.

"What are you doing on school grounds without authorization?" asked the bald guy.

"Well might we ask you?" said Pongo again.

Jake wheeled up to Pongo. "What does that even mean?"

"Whatever it means," said Ben, "it doesn't sound as good the second time."

"Ssshhh!" hissed Pongo. "I'm trying to interrogate baldy here."

"Baldy?" said the bald guy. "What do you mean, baldy?"

"Well might we—"

"Not again," interrupted Jake. "You sound like a complete doofus."

"What's going on?" asked one of the really, *really* bad guys in the bright orange jacket. "Who are you guys?"

"Well might—" began Pongo before Ben stuffed a shuriken in his mouth.

"*We* ask the questions," said Jake, withdrawing his sword and clipping the bald guy over the head with it.

"OUCH!" said the bald guy.

"There's plenty more where that came from, baldy," said Jake.

"Jake Chen, Pongo Twistleton, Veejay Cameron and Ben Clarkeson!" snapped the bald guy, whose voice now seemed strangely familiar. And it was around this time the Nerdy Ninjas began to regret not wearing their itchy masks.

"You guessed our names? That's a pretty clever trick, baldy," said Pongo, spitting out the shuriken and finally finding something to say other than, "Well might we ask you?"

Veejay clipped the bald guy again.

"OUCH!" he said. "Veejay Cameron. Stop that immediately. Surely your mother would disapprove of your clipping!"

"How do you know our names?" asked Ben. He gave the bald guy another poke.

"Ben Clarkeson!" said the bald guy. "See me in my office first thing Monday morning!"

"Who are you?" said Jake. He gave the bald guy another clip, just for good measure.

"I'm your principal!" snapped the bald guy.

The four ninjas stared at the bald guy.

"Mr. Kinkoffen?" said Ben.

"Indeed," said ~~the bald guy~~ Mr. Kinkoffen.

"Riiiight," said Ben, finally figuring it out.

weird bald dude   **mr. kinkoffen!**

"But . . . but . . . what are you doing here on the weekend?" asked Pongo.

Mr. Kinkoffen stared at Pongo. *"Well might I ask you?"*

"And what happened to your hair?" said Jake.

"It's in my office," said Mr. Kinkoffen.

"Why?" asked Veejay, not unreasonably. "Did it have something better to do?"

"Because I didn't put it on this morning!" scoffed Mr. Kinkoffen.

"You mean you wear a wig?" asked Veejay.

"Forget that," said Pongo. "These three guys here—in the orange—were going to blow up Brandon House! We've thwarted their wicked plans!"

"Blow up Brandon House? I know that!" snapped Mr. Kinkoffen. "I'm the one who hired them!"

"So you're in on it too!" said Ben.

Veejay was about to clip Mr. Kinkoffen again, but fortunately for him some sort of primitive survival instinct kicked in and he decided not to. Plus his mother *had* warned him against clipping people (and animals).

"You're in with these really *really* bad guys?" said Jake.

"They're *not* bad guys," said Mr. Kinkoffen as the bad guys started snickering. "They're demolition experts."

"Ha ha!" said Ben in a sort of "got you" voice.

"As you know," continued Mr. Kinkoffen, "Brandon House has been unstable for many years. A bit like Colonel Brandon himself. So the St. Hall's board decided to have it demolished and rebuilt on the same site. Didn't you see

the fluoro green caution tape cordoning off the perimeter?"

"Ohhhh," said Pongo. "I thought that was the new handball area."

"But they said," Veejay pointed to the really, *really* bad guys (or "demolition experts" as they preferred to be called), "that they were also going to *take care* of the rest of the school."

Mr. Kinkoffen shook his head. "Yes! There are further repairs needed around the school! These gentlemen are involved in those maintenance jobs. You want the toilets improved, don't you?"

"Oh, riiiight," said Ben.

"Oops," said Jake.

"Are we in trouble, sir?" said Pongo.

"They made me do it," said Veejay. The other three glared at him.

"You know something, boys," said Mr. Kinkoffen, "it's one thing to be on the school grounds during the weekend without authorization. It's quite another to clip your principal repeatedly with rolled up newspapers. Release us at once!"

For a moment the ninjas considered clipping Mr. Kinkoffen repeatedly some more. But that would be dishonorable and was not the way of the ninja. Instead they slowly, reluctantly, untied their principal and the three really *really* bad demolition experts.

"Wait a minute," said Jake, as he watched the demolition expert with the beard sneak over to his tarp-covered wheelbarrow. "You! You're hiding something in there, aren't you?"

"Er, um—" the bearded expert began. "No, I—"

"Don't be so ridiculous, Mr. Chen," scoffed Mr. Kinkoffen. "He has absolutely nothing to hide. Haven't you boys caused enough trouble today?"

"I don't believe it," said Jake. "You might not have planned on blowing up our school for no good reason, but you are hiding something in there, I'm sure of it!" Jake leaned out of his chair and pushed the wheelbarrow over with one great heave.

The wheelbarrow clanged to the ground

loudly, sending the contents spilling out from under the blue tarp.

Out tumbled a mountain of books! School books!

"A-ha!" said Pongo, bouncing excitedly on the spot. "Jake was right! You are a thief! You've stolen books from St. Hall's Hall Library!"

Mr. Kinkoffen bent down slowly and picked up two of the books. "*Swan Lake?*" he asked the demolition expert curiously. "*Blending Ballet Basics with Ballistics?*"

"Er . . . um . . . I . . ."

"Explain yourself!" said Jake.

"I, er, um . . ." said the expert, nervously tugging his beard. "Well I really love blowing stuff up," he said, "don't get me wrong. But what I really *really* love is . . . **BALLET**! I've always wanted to be a ballerina! After I'd learned a few leaps and pirouettes I was going to return the books to the school, I swear!"

With that, the bearded, wheelbarrow-pushing demolition expert / thief / ballerina-wannabe, lifted his hard hat and leapt up into a graceful triple-twirl.

Jake, Pongo, Ben, Mr. Kinkoffen and the other two demolition experts looked on, dumbfounded.

"OH, BRAVO!" sang Veejay, clapping enthusiastically. **"BRAVO!"**

12

THE ~~end of the~~ NERDY NINJAS

A ninja is advised to retire and put away his shurikens when his passion to do good is gone and he feels that he can no longer jump backwards into trees without the aid of a trampoline or rocket boots. After this, ninja lawn bowls is recommended.

The Ninja Warrior's Handbook, Volume 27

The four nerdy ninjas sat forlornly in their secret hideout. Even though they'd successfully uncovered a serious school property theft (and even though Ben had complained that his father had an important squash game that night), Mr. Kinkoffen had insisted on confiscating their swords and shurikens.

"Can you believe it?" said Jake. "Two hundred years on detention."

"And we're not allowed to be ninjas anymore," said Ben.

Pongo shook his head. "That's so unfair."

"What?" said Veejay. "Two hundred years on detention?"

"No," said Pongo. "That we can't be ninjas anymore."

"Are we really going to listen to him?" asked Jake.

Everyone looked at Jake. Could they disobey Mr. Kinkoffen? Did they really want to run the risk of adding to their detention sentence?

"He can tell us what to do at school," continued Jake, "but he can't tell us what to do in our own time."

"Jake's right," said Pongo. "We are going to continue with our missions. Because you know what, chaps?"

"Chaps?" said Jake, Ben and Veejay in unison.

"Okay then," said Pongo. "Because you know what, **GUYS**?"

"What?" they said.

"We're going to carry on as we have been because someday, somewhere, someone is going to need a ninja, or *four* . . . whether they know it or not."

The other three nodded in agreement.

Pongo put his outstretched hand in the middle of the group. "The Nerdy Ninjas!"

Jake, Ben and Veejay put their hands on top of his. **"THE NERDY NINJAS!"** they said together.

Right at that moment a blood-curdling scream came shrilling out from the forest . . .

Veejay gulped. "What was that?"

"Probably just a vampire," said Jake.

"A vampire?" said Veejay. "You're not allowed

to talk about vampires in my presence—it's in my list!" he added, pulling out the infamous note (book) once more.

"Yeah," said Jake, ignoring the reams of paper now filling the tree house. "There's been a steady increase in vampire activity in the suburb lately. It was in the local paper. Just after the article about that woman who complained about the neighbors' dogs barking. Come on, Veejay . . . this sounds like a job for—"

"THE NERDY NINJAS!" said the four friends again.

"But remember," said Veejay. "I'm not allowed to cross the road and I have to be home by seven."

To be continued . . .

ACKNOWLEDGMENTS

Shogun would like to pay his respect to the staff, students and ninjas of Knox Grammar school. He would like to express his eternal gratitude to Ben Close for rescuing him from the perilous state of non-existence. To Wendy Lim and Matt Brooker for that unforgettable conversation that led to the ninjas. Thanks to Peter "Caruthers" Brandon for his glares. Thanks also to Susie Bottomley for being Susie Bottomley, Ana Vivas for starting the whole thing off, and to Rebecca Young-san, editor, colleague, ninja.